SHERMAN'S
CHAPLAIN

SHERMAN'S CHAPLAIN

DAVID BELLIN

EPIGRAPH BOOKS
RHINEBECK, NY

Printed in the United States of America

Book and cover design by Joe Tantillo

Epigraph Books
22 E. Market Street, Suite 304
Rhinebeck, New York 12572
www.epigraphPS.com
USA 845-876-4861

Hardcover ISBN 978-1-9369400-2-8
Softcover   ISBN 978-1-9369400-1-1

Library of Congress Control Number: 2011924838

*For Kristen, this century's embodiment
of Proverbs 31:10-31*

Although inspired by incidents during the Union Army's march from Atlanta to Savannah (Nov. 1864-Jan. 1865), *Sherman's Chaplain* is a work of fiction.

Imaginary characters mingle with historical figures. Most locations are authentic but some are invented. Dates are generally accurate but some have been adjusted to preserve narrative flow. All conversations in the book are the author's invention. Among the fictional characters, any resemblance to persons living or dead is purely coincidental.

CONTENTS

CHAPTER ONE:

THE PROMOTION

November 30, 1864

My Dearest Elaine,

This is no jest. A short while ago, I sat alone with General Sherman on a moonlit bluff examining a town below called Hillardville, Georgia. I assume we'll capture it tomorrow or the next day and I don't know what is expected of me when it happens. I'm weary, my dearest, after a long day and night, but will tell you as much as I can before sleep overtakes me.

Yes, that general, William Tecumseh himself. How did somebody two months out of seminary, assigned as a mere regimental chaplain, end up the lone companion of the general who commands all of our Southern armies? I can only call it God's will, materializing in the form of a mounted sergeant from headquarters, galloping into our company ground last Sunday morning.

I had been preparing to preach, nerves on edge. It was the first time in the field, the first time before battle-hardened men. Adding to the burden, of course, was the stain on the reputation of chaplains left by the rogues and pretenders. There's no doubt most chaplains were selfless men of God who served with bravery but when you have some who steal or drink and gamble, their stories are the ones that command attention. An artillery lieutenant spoke of a chaplain, an ordained Baptist preacher, who pushed his way into a poker game, came away with all the cash and then flaunted the stack of bills around the regiment. The lieutenant related that at lunch in a good ringing voice so all could hear.

Given stories like that, and the fact that I had never seen battle, the men were generally scornful of me. It showed in a narrow glance, a turn of the back, an off-color story deliberately told in my hearing, lack of help with a blanket roll or a saddle (they helped each other instantly without a word) and, most depressing on this first Sunday morning, a mere handful of men sitting on the grassy hill where I planned to preach. Even the regimental officers were missing.

That changed rapidly when the sergeant raced in, yelling, "Uncle Billy's coming, Uncle Billy's coming for church!" Uncle Billy is Sherman and it turned out he was camped just two miles away. The rider dashed over to me. "Headquarters chaplain got the dysentery so they're coming here. Better preach up a storm, brother!"

In minutes, the hill was covered with men jammed so close you couldn't get another body in, except for the space left in front for Sherman and his officers, about a dozen of them. The crowd spilled over the sides of the hill and some men even lodged in the trees. They're a cavalier group, this army so far from home. At first glance, their Union blue overcoats and sack coats give a military look, a semblance of uniformity. Then the eye catches the varied colors of the shirts beneath the coats, the many-hued patches on trousers and the assortment of head coverings perched at individual angles—forage caps, high-crowned felt hats, round "coal scuttle" caps, even a fez on a man wrapped over a tree limb. One thing they have in common, though, are boots and shoes of leather in good repair. They say Sherman looks at feet, not frills, one of the many reasons he's earned their loyalty.

Their faces are something else they have in common. Although the men vary in age from downy-faced youths to stubbled old-timers, in unguarded moments they all show

---

the same wintry resolve and the same deepset eyes staring out the message, I've seen the worst and I can abide it.

Most often, though, it's the jubilance that shows, evident in a careless stride, almost a swagger, as they perform even the mundane tasks of cleaning weapons and washing clothes; evident, too, in oft-repeated, eager questions: "When do we move out?" "When do we chase the Rebs again?"

They're fresh from the capture of Atlanta, which is probably part of it, but even more, there's Sherman. I'm convinced he's the catalyst for their jubilance. You could sense how much they wanted to yell and cheer when he cantered into sight. They held themselves to a murmur, a deep-throated sound that swelled like a wave and slowly quieted, only because it was a Sunday and this was a surrogate church and there was a man with a Bible facing them, about to deliver the word of God.

You may correctly assume the word of God was in terrified hands at that instant. It was not the size of the gathering; indeed, I had preached to larger assemblages in seminary training. It was Sherman, a man now celebrated around the world, settling into a camp chair not twenty feet away. His rumpled jacket and shapeless hat told me why his army was not fussy about uniforms but that caught my attention only in passing. It was the craggy face that transfixed me, the face so familiar from newspaper photographs and sketches, except photographs and sketches cannot capture the impact of aging that war inflicts on a man, and it's terribly pronounced on Sherman. You would call him a man in his sixties if you didn't know he was twenty years younger.

I might be staring still if a soldier hadn't come over with ammunition boxes to stand on, a little platform I would need now that there was a crowd to address. As they were set up, I realized Sherman was studying my face as I had studied his. He was expressionless, making me wonder if I had gaped like a schoolboy at him. The thought added to my trepidation and I stepped up on the platform slowly, determined not to stumble, and determined to begin in a loud and confident tone. The general and the men here knew all about warfare, I told myself, but I knew all about the word of God. In short, this army was on my territory now.

I took a deep breath and straightened up, opening my Bible, ready to declaim the opening words of Nehemiah with the strong and deep voice projection we had learned so well in class. I was pleased when we bivouacked by this little hill. It was thickly wooded on three sides with live oak that would deaden other sounds, and with God's hand at work, a mild breeze arose at my back to help carry my words.

All public speakers know the instruction to look silently at the audience for a few seconds before starting, a way to secure attention. I followed the advice, letting my eyes roam around the ranks, stealing another glance at the preternaturally aged Sherman. I was grateful that I did and suddenly grateful, too, for the many seminary exercises in speaking spontaneously.

With words from the Book of James in my head, "God giveth grace to the humble," I closed the Bible and placed it carefully under my arm. There was a stirring on the hill and an inquiring tilt of the head from Sherman. I said, directly to him but loud enough for all to hear, "Sir, my name is Ellis Brantley. I'm the regimental chaplain here and I believe a man must earn his way in this world."

I looked at the crowd and repeated, "I believe a man must earn his way in this world." I gestured from one side of the hill to the other and went on, biting the words into a slow, even cadence.

"Everyone here has earned his way. You have earned it fighting. You have earned it in the pain of injuries. You have earned it through the grief of seeing brothers and cousins and dear friends die violently. You have earned it shivering in the cold and sweltering in the heat. You have earned it suffering illness and disease. You have earned it slogging through swamps, marching endless roads, climbing hill after hill. You have earned it going hungry—and do you know where I was while you were doing all that?"

I waited for an answer. It took a while in the constraining presence of the commanding general, but finally one of the bolder ones shouted, "You was being rocked in yo' cradle, snug and safe." A wave of laughter rolled across the hill and even Sherman and his officers wore faint smiles.

I grinned at the speaker. "Even better, I was in a seminary." Another wave of laughter rolled, punctuated with derisive hoots. You know that seminaries are regarded as havens for those seeking to delay or avoid the army and that ramshackle seminaries, run by clerics in name only, have sprung up like dandelions.

I let the laughter fade and my smile fade and said, "I graduated from Calvary Seminary in Provincetown, Rhode Island. It's eighty-eight years old and you study hard there, twelve hours a day, six days a week, for four years. So it's a genuine place of learning, devoted to the gospel of Jesus Christ.

"But the truth is, the rooms are warm and dry and we get three good meals a day and there isn't a Rebel army within four hundred miles. So I'm the one man here who did not earn his way into this camp, this hill, this army. There are places that are burned into your memory—Fort Donelson, Cairo, Shiloh, Vicksburg, Chickasaw Bluffs, Chattanooga, Kennesaw Mountain—real places for you and they are only names to me.

"So if you want to say, Chaplain Brantley, what gives you the right to stand here before a great fighting general and a great fighting army and talk to us man to man, I would say I do not have that right—except there is a battlefield that is only a name to you, but it is a real place to me."

I took the Bible from under my arm. "That place is Jerusalem. That place is Jerusalem in the days of Nehemia. Invasion after invasion has destroyed the city. The walls of Jerusalem look like the walls of Vicksburg today, just rubble. When Nehemia walks on those walls, when he steps on those broken, battered stones, I walk with him. I feel each stone, sharp and painful beneath my feet. And I want you to feel it the same way."

And then I delivered the Nehemia sermon I know by heart, the one you may know by heart, too, from the many times you were my practice audience. It went well, the men absorbing attentively the story of God's call to rebuild the walls and Nehemia's faithfulness and strength in overcoming his enemies. Soft calls arose of "Amen," and "Tell it, brother," and I knew, but for the high-ranking officers in attendance, there would have been the resounding shouts of approval one hears from a fired-up congregation.

Sherman himself sat thoughtfully throughout, then he and his aides stood up with a scraping of camp chairs and left without a word, a disappointment until the commander of my own regiment came to me and said, "The general enjoyed that sermon."

"How do you know?" I asked.

"Because he sat without fidgeting, because when one of the colonels started to whisper something to him, he shushed the fellow so he could pay attention to you. I know Uncle Billy. You did well."

As for the rank and file, I didn't need to hear anything

second-hand. More men than I could count clapped me on the shoulder or called out words of praise: "Made me feel at home, Parson," "I'll be with you every Sunday, Chaplain," "You raised me up, thank the Lord," and the one I prize the most, the old-timer who measured me up and down, rubbed his gray chin whiskers in thought, then decided, "You preach as good as the best of them. You'll go far, sonny."

The narrow glances were now replaced by friendly ones and backs were no longer turned when I came by. I felt pleased and, I must confess, I had to work hard to stamp out a touch of vanity. I reminded myself that those words of James, "God giveth grace to the humble," are preceded by, "God resisteth the proud."

I must give way to sleep now and will resume, with God's help, in the morning. I'll continue in the narrative style of this letter, presuming it's what you meant when you said, "Make it a story." You're probably catering to my illusion that I can write like Sir Walter Scott while I preach like John Wesley. What pretentiousness. Goodnight, my dearest.

With deep love and devotion,
Ellis

December 1, 1864

My Dearest Elaine,

I'm rested after a night of sleeping on a cot instead of a bedroll, in a tent large enough to hold not only the cot but a canvas camp chair and a collapsible table. It's a state of relative luxury that does not keep me from missing you painfully. I have had my morning devotions, praying and reading in Lamentations, but I must confess you were in my thoughts as much as the word of our Lord. Blasphemy, surely. And love and longing for you just as surely, driven by an urgent need for your reassurance. You see, I am now chaplain for the general staff of one of Sherman's armies, more than fifty weathered officers, and the enlisted men who serve them.

Their appointed chaplain, the one I preached for, turned delirious with fever the next day, obviously suffering more than just dysentery, and was hurried off to hospital in Chattanooga. Sherman summoned me instantly and so here I am, in his headquarters, although they're not actually his and, while he is at hand right now, he often will be absent. If you have been following the newspapers, you know that Sherman leads two armies: this one, called the Army of Georgia, and a counterpart, the Army of the Tennessee that moves roughly parallel, ranging from twenty to fifty miles away. Sherman rides between with a cavalry squad for escort, coordinating the two forces and, according to the men, "keeping his office in his pocket."

The result is that he has no real headquarters but bunks with whichever of the two commands he lights at, in this case the command of Major General John Slocum. The other army is commanded by Major General Oliver Otis Howard, a one-armed general (he lost his right arm at Seven Pines) who takes his Bible everywhere and exhorts his men to pray each morning and attend services. The men call him "Old Prayerbook." Would I have been happier there? It would have meant more respect, but also more pressure. I believe I would have felt Howard's eyes on me everywhere, like living with a seminary headmaster again. At all events, the Lord has brought me here and I'm content to be with Slocum, a man of no outward religious display. He nodded when we were introduced and has ignored me since.

And that is why, my beloved, your recent seminary graduate is abruptly living in the fine accommodations of a senior chaplain. I even inherited his orderly, a corporal named Lambert, about my age but with the veteran's easygoing cynicism. I asked him how the chaplain had spent his time.

"Mostly visitin' with the other officers here, sir, but ain't no point you tryin' to do that, all of them veterans and you never seen no combat. You can just laze around 'cept for Sunday. And of course when the fightin' starts again, you'll have the funerals. Would you like this?" he added, handing me a shiny little brass crucifix. "Last chaplain used to wear these, left this one behind."

I considered the authorized chaplain's uniform I wore—plain black frock coat with a meager row of brass buttons up the front, black trousers, round-brimmed black hat—and I considered the creativity of dress in this army. I thanked Lambert and pinned on the cross. After spending some time thinking and praying about Lambert's views on how to spend my time, I made up my mind to institute morning prayers and evening Bible study. Out of this big headquarters, somebody was bound to show up and where two or more gather in His name...

By dusk, I was halfway through preparing a simple study course, one that could be interrupted in times of combat, when Sherman's messenger—the sergeant who had come galloping into camp—peered into the tent.

"Uncle Billy wants you, Preacher. Better get a fresh horse."

"Where are we going?"

"Scouting."

"That's cavalry work. I don't know anything about it."

"Uncle Billy knows everything about it. You're along for company."

Two hours later, we were on that moonlit bluff I mentioned, nobody else in sight, after a slow trot through pine woods chilled with the approach of winter. The trail was rough and dark, rising and twisting, but Sherman kept a steady gait ahead of me and I simply stayed in his wake.

My confidence was helped by the knowledge that a mounted squad followed a short distance behind. Sherman tried to do these scouting missions by himself, the sergeant had told me, taking along just one other person to act as messenger if needed, usually, like me, the newest member of the staff. However, the men were not about to allow their beloved Uncle Billy to go unprotected, orders or not.

He knew it, grunting softly at a crackling of underbrush back on the trail while edging his stallion out to the rim of the ridge for a full view of Hillardville, revealed below in soft patterns of shadow and moonlight. Practiced eyes scoured streets and courtyards, roofs and verandas, a small park with a bandstand, a white frame church with a squat steeple. A mill house and a glassy stream that fed it marked the far edge of town. A single railroad track flanked the mill, curved north to a small depot platform and a nearby feed house and glinted away into the darkness. After a full minute of study, he said, "Why must they always look so peaceful?"

"Moonlight can do that," I suggested, instinctively shrinking down in the saddle. Our voices were loud in the still air and we were silhouetted targets on the bluff.

Somehow he noticed, although his eyes hadn't left the town. "Nobody's threatening us," he said. With deliberation, he took a cigar and a matchbox from his saddlebag and puffed the cigar into a glow that looked like a searchlight beacon to me.

"Never been near any fighting, have you?"

"No, sir. I joined just a month ago."

"You get to feel when you're being observed. This town's just sitting still. Which doesn't mean they're unaware of us." He swiveled to regard me. "It's not moonlight, Parson. It's defeat that makes it look so peaceful. Think that through."

I gazed over the roofs again, imagining the reports of Sherman's advance reaching the town week after week, the burning, the destruction and the shock—still raw—of the devastation visited upon Atlanta.

"Like a whipped animal?"

"Like a whipped animal. Too fearful to stir, hoping if it doesn't move you won't notice it. All the men fit to fight are gone. We might run into one or two of the older men, or even a woman, with some spark left, maybe try to shoot at us from a window or behind a barn." He pointed down at vantage points invisible to me. "I admire it. I dread it."

"Is that why towns get burned?"

He fingered the horse's mane silently. When he replied, his voice was weary. "Somebody shoots from a barn, that barn's going to go up in flames, and the house and property that go with it and maybe houses close by, maybe more, a whole town. Fire spreads. Men protecting themselves can be hard to rein in."

"Just protecting themselves?" I said without thinking. The words hung a little caustically in the night air and I regretted them but he replied with no annoyance.

"How many Scripture verses are there about vengeance belonging to the Lord? A dozen?"

"At least."

"And if you preached on them it would be a hair-raiser—you've got the gift—but the men of this army would miss your meaning altogether."

I simply looked at him.

"Think it through, Parson."

"Well, everybody knows the verse from Romans Twelve, 'Dearly beloved, avenge not yourselves'—oh."

"Yes, you're seeing it."

"They believe they're doing the Lord's work?"

"Our officers pray and call on God's help when they lead their men into battle. The newspapers say preserving the Union is a holy crusade. Politicians make speeches about the godless enemy. Abolitionists tell us slavery is an offense to Christianity " He pointed downward. "Look at the church."

I glanced down at the white-painted walls and the square, short steeple.

"It may be gone tomorrow, torn apart timber by timber, pew by pew. Churches make fine firewood, did you know that? The only building in town kept warm and dry all the time and the benches come out easily. The point is this: the men aren't thinking, 'I'm tearing down a church.' They're thinking, 'I'm tearing down a Rebel church.'"

"It can't look any different than the churches they went to at home."

"In those churches, people pray for their safety. In these churches, people pray for their death and damnation. How can God be pleased with such a place? So it's God's hand that's taking it down and nothing you can say will change that."

I looked again at the church, sorrowful, seeing it in ruins, vaguely hearing Sherman's voice, then growing even more heartsore as the words penetrated.

"I don't discourage that attitude, Parson."

He reined the horse around, expecting no answer and, of course, I had none to give. He was calm, even fatherly, but a general had warned the most junior member of his command and no discussion was in order. And I understood. He led armies that, for all their might, were treading alone in a hostile land. With no supply lines and the nearest reinforcements a three-week march away, the Army of Georgia and the Army of the Tennessee were marching, foraging, fighting and winning all on their own.

The strategy was daring and heavy with risk. To make it work, the army must not only be remorseless, it must be perceived that way. Sherman is clearly a decent man. There was wistfulness in his question, "Why must they always look so peaceful?" I'm sure he'll restrain the wildest of the troops, the house-burners and looters, as well as he can. It was said he did that at Atlanta once military targets were demolished. But vengeance against the person and property of any one who shoots or even threatens the soldiers, or the willful turning of a church into firewood—there will be no restraint there. The army needs the relief and the general needs to feed the fear of his enemies.

Pray for the hours ahead. When we returned, Lambert told me the orders had been given to move into Hillardville in the morning.

My mind is full, darling Elaine, and my soul is heavy. I turn to our Lord for his mercy on the innocents in Hillardville and the army descending on them.

Your devoted and loving,
Ellis

CHAPTER TWO:

HILLARDVILLE

December 2, 1864

My Dearest Elaine,

I know so little of this war. I wrote last of the army descending on Hillardville and if my words made it seem that the entire Army of Georgia would roll down like an avalanche, that was the misty picture in my mind.

The reality is that one terrified Negro man led the way into Hillardville. Stooped and elderly, outfitted in a crumpled Confederate officer's hat, an oversize Union army shirt that hung to his knees and ragged britches that revealed bony shins and bare feet, he staggered into Hillardville under the weight of a bass drum. Painted on the drum was a Union flag.

I had seen three grinning troopers strap the drum to the poor fellow when I left my tent this morning. You've heard, I'm sure, how slaves leave their plantations and farms to follow the army, some of the men hoping vainly to join while others, often whole families, simply seek food or a protected way north, with no understanding of the geography involved. It's impossible to discourage them and so there are always Negroes available for hauling and digging or, in this case, a sad and cruel humiliation of the residents of Hillardville. Sad and cruel, and inhuman to the Negro. The sight could easily rub emotions so raw that some resident would shoot him, whatever the consequences.

Having said that, I must confess to my Creator that there is, no matter how I fight it, a wisp of satisfaction at humiliating the enemy. They are the slave owners, they

14

are the ones who started this war, and the acid humor of sending this lone colored slave to herald the fall of their village satisfies some primal need. I understand Sherman's men and their urge to vengeance a little better, except that I offer myself to the world as a man of God and, inwardly and outwardly, I should be a complete model of God's grace and love.

I made an attempt. If you call it weak, you are justified. I walked over to the three men and the Negro. Lambert, my orderly, and a few mounted officers were nearby. Behind them, soldiers were milling around, those in front watching the action, chatting and laughing. Others in the field beyond were forming ranks. I noticed a regimental flag—only one—meaning about three hundred men were assembling.

I saluted the officers and one of them, a captain, said "Good morning, Chaplain," as he returned the salute. There was a suspicious edge to it.

Lambert stepped towards me. "Good day to you, Parson. Ever seen anything like this before?" He was deliberately cheerful and just as deliberately in my path.

"Never did," I replied taking his arm and turning him to walk beside me. "Tell me what's happening." My legs trembled a bit under me but I think my grip on Lambert was firm. At least he stayed at my side and explained the obvious.

"This old fella's goin' into town for us. Goin' ahead of the troops to announce us. It's a merciful thing to do, give warnin' and all." As we reached the scene, Lambert finished pointedly, "He's a volunteer."

I became aware of the piercing musky odor one associates with colored people, more invasive here than usual, no doubt made sharper by fear. He glistened with sweat, even in the morning chill, a gaunt fellow with a markedly broad, flat nose and lips that were thick even for his race. I was sure these pronounced African features played a part in his selection.

The three troopers moved into a tighter knot around him so that I had to peer between them. I noticed sergeant's stripes on the arm next to me and looked at the owner, a stocky fellow watching me with thin-lipped irritation.

"Good morning, Sergeant. What's this fellow's name?"

"G'mawning. His name, must be, ah, Mose. That the name he answered to?" he asked the other two.

One of them said, "Yup," and the other spread his palms to indicate "Who cares?"

I edged myself closer to the Negro. "That your name? Mose?"

He glanced at me blankly, nodded once, then peered at the ground. It was clear he would agree with anything he was asked. Nevertheless, I persevered.

"This is a brave thing you're doing. Is it what you want to do?"

He repeated the single nod without looking at me this time.

"I'm the headquarters chaplain," I said. "A preacher. You can tell me the truth. If you don't want to do this, you can tell me."

He remained mute, no nod, eyes down. I tried one more time. "Did you hear me? You can tell me if you don't want to do this."

Again, he stood mute.

I heard the shuffle of horses and knew the officers had moved closer. The silence beyond them told me the soldiers in the front ranks, the talkers and laughers, were now quiet, observing. I felt the rough pressure of the troopers on either side and heard Lambert breathing noisily at my back. This was the moment to break into the small circle, unbuckle the drum, face the officers and declare that they were doing something unfitting for Christian men, then escort the poor Negro to headquarters, marching straight through the resentful ranks to confront Sherman.

Or this was the moment to give it up and go back to my tent, excused from any action by the Negro's unresponsiveness.

I chose a third course, one that would avoid confrontation yet appease my conscience, or so I told myself.

"Let us bow in prayer," I said quietly to the little group. I felt a rustle of surprise, but heads went down. For the next few seconds at least, I held them captive.

"Our heavenly Father, we ask for thy blessing on this army as it moves forward once again. We thank thee for thy shield of protection over those who have fought so bravely for so long, and who are sworn to continue the battle, no matter the danger, for the cause so dear to their hearts. And we pray for the citizens of Hillardille, that they will heed the warning they are about to receive."

I took a breath. Then, more slowly, "And for the one who carries the warning, this humble servant marching alone into peril, hold him in thy merciful hand as lovingly as thou held the prophets of old."

Only Lambert uttered an audible "Amen." The others grunted and the sergeant even jostled me, with intent, I suspect, as he and the other two re-formed around the Negro.

The man had now lifted his head and stared directly at me. His lips moved, forming a word I couldn't make out. Then his eyes lifted to the sky and back to me and I understood: he was trying to thank me.

Nothing could have shamed me more.

I will tell you in my next letter of events that followed in Hillardville. I cannot go on without turning once again to our Creator for His forgiveness.

Your devoted and unworthy,
Ellis

December 3, 1864

My Dearest Elaine,

I tried to ride with the vanguard following the Negro into Hillardville, a cavalry unit of about thirty in two wide and straight ranks, the men patting at their brows with their kerchiefs. The day was turning unusually warm, one of those summer-like December days one encounters here.

As I lined up, the major in charge glanced at me in surprise that turned to exasperation. I recognized him as one of the spectators when I prayed for the Negro.

"This is a battlefield situation, Chaplain. You need to stay with the wagons."

I trotted slowly to the rear, thinking of the poor old fellow on his way to town. "Battlefield situation," I muttered. Still, I reminded myself, if only one rash Hillardville resident fired a gun, the bullet could kill or maim. To the man struck, one round was battlefield enough.

I examined faces among the infantry marchers as I rode, imagining this man with the rough beard or that one with the long jaw suddenly struck, falling, trying to summon for my untried senses the corrosive shock of battle as these men knew it. But in truth, the scene was nonchalant enough, the men barely noticing me as they whispered among themselves in what seemed a happy and expectant stir, more than the mere taking of a town would warrant. I noticed, too, that this one regiment of three hundred would be the entire force.

I pulled up next to a wagon driven by a corporal and a private, both no more than eighteen years old, if that. They gave me a cheery, "Mornin' Parson," and I was relieved to realize neither of them, being in the rear, would have observed my encounter with the Negro.

"Morning, men. Are these all the troops we're sending to take the town?"

They both laughed and the corporal said, "Now don't worry none, Parson. Half o' these would be enough."

The private leaned over, acting confidential, and said, "Fact is, on a normal day we'd be sendin' in a lot more just for the exercise. But today's different." He looked at the other for confirmation.

"Well, words goin' round that General Joe Wheeler and his Reb cavalry is entrenchin' up ahead—"

"Place called Danner's Crossing," inserted the private.

"And they got some infantry from some kind of military academy, so we're sendin' three regiments to hit 'em hard and others to cut off retreat and maybe a couple more to flank 'em—"

"Thinks he's Uncle Billy," laughed the private. "Tryin' to strategize."

"Well, I wish he'd-a sent us. But leastways we'll have some fun in town." He pointed to the back of the wagon.

I looked around to see picks, shovels, iron-headed mallets and long crowbars filling the cargo space.

"Mostly it's the railroad tracks we tear up, but along the way, you know." He grinned.

I knew he meant the town itself. "You'll spare the church, won't you, boys?" I asked.

19

The corporal chewed his lip thoughtfully for a moment, then responded, "Oh, sure, Parson. If you want to take some things for yourself, we'll wait 'til you finish. But the gold and silver things and them old Bibles with the gilted-up covers, you won't find none. They take 'em away 'fore we ever get near."

I groaned inwardly. "I didn't mean souvenirs for myself. It's the church. I don't like to see a church destroyed."

They looked at each other and then the private, with surprising gentleness, said, "It's just another Reb house, Parson. A church? Well, the chaplain who was here 'fore you told us a true church could be in a tent or a barn or just outside." He waved at the hills. "Like when you preached to Uncle Billy t'other day," he concluded, pleased with this validation of the point.

The troops ahead had now started to march and the corporal clucked his horses into motion. The wagon creaked and rattled, joined by other supply and ammunition wagons around us and the din erased any chance I might have had to carry on the debate.

The incline leading to Hillardville lay before us and I decided the major would probably be too busy to care about me the rest of the way. I was eager to get close enough to the front to slip into town and, tapping the horse into a quick walk, I eased without difficulty into the ranks. The troops were accustomed to mounted officers among them on the attack and very few bothered to look up at the rider. In time, I was close enough to the front to see the cavalry unit and I reined back into a gait that would keep the distance between us.

We had been descending a sloping field abutting the bluff where I sat with Sherman (only last night, I marveled), a field of scrub brush and bristly brown November grass that funneled into the road to Hillardville.

Suddenly, that posed a dilemma: the troops would soon have to close their columns into the limited space offered by the road. If I stayed among them the horse and I would be a hindrance. If I sped into the open, I would be in the "battlefield situation" the major had forbidden me to enter.

There was a moment of panic, a murmured prayer for wisdom, then I spurred the animal ahead.

My darling Elaine, you know me as no other person in this world does. I hold nothing back from you and so, with embarrassment, I tell you I felt a thrill while charging forward. The wind at my face, the beast sturdy and fast beneath me—well, I will not grow too lyrical about it, but I know why men join the cavalry. I can see you shaking your head, saying, "Ellis, Ellis, Ellis." I join you in shaking my head and saying, "Ellis, Ellis, Ellis."

We have a God of infinite compassion, though, and He chose to shield a fool. Just as I passed the first row of marchers, the confines of the road forced the major and his cavalry out of their neatly aligned ranks into a stretched and irregular file. It easily concealed an extra rider and I fell in at the rear without notice.

The unit re-formed when we entered the silent main thoroughfare of Hillardville, splitting into a parade of two columns, one on each side of the way, riders stiff-backed, looking neither left nor right, demonstrating the confidence of the victorious. The quick-step thudding of the approaching infantry made clear the vengeance that any attack on the cavalry would provoke.

Several large houses lined the way, of brick or of wood frame painted in fresh-looking shades of yellow and peach, set back behind shade trees and flower gardens now thinned by autumn. A broad veranda spanned the front of every house, enclosed either by a waist-high, latticed brick ledge or by delicate ironwork. The street ended in a small park and bandstand to the left and the church to the right, as I had seen from the bluff, although the church was more massive from this angle, a bulky structure dwarfing the houses and almost shiny in its whiteness. Beyond, I recalled, lay other homes, small and ramshackle compared to this part of the town, then the mill house, the stream, and the now-doomed railroad tracks.

Facing the last house before the park was the Negro, straining to hold up the drum, an even more forlorn figure than earlier. The major and two officers ignored him as they rode past to see the farther side of town, leaving the rest of their unit to manage the foot soldiers and the residents. These officers now began to lounge in their saddles, opening collar buttons, lighting pipes or cigars, paying no more attention to the Negro than the major did; the old fellow had served his purpose.

Riding to the end of the street, drawing a contemptuous headshake from one of the officers, I saw the Negro incline his head deeply, almost a bow, and walk heavily around the side of the house. I realized he had been talking to someone on the porch but it was empty when I got there. As I pondered whether to follow him or find the person he spoke to, the infantry columns arrived and started to fill the street with a noisy tumult.

Following the Negro around the side of the house at this point would make it look as if I were trying to sneak in, confirming the image of chaplain-as-looter. I tied the horse to a shrub and marched firmly up the steps to a front door of scrolled oak, highly burnished. A window to one side was covered with a damask curtain that stirred as I knocked.

When no one responded, I tried several times again, each time more forcefully. Finally, I faced the curtained window, stretched my arms to show I carried no weapon, buffed up the gold cross on my lapel and pointed to it. The curtain moved and a boy of about twelve, dark-haired and sullen, looked at the cross, looked at me, then called out to someone inside.

The door opened and a woman slipped out, closing the door swiftly to make sure I couldn't take stock of anything behind her. From her hair and features, she was clearly the boy's mother, although sullenness in him had ripened to indignation in her.

"Are you here to laugh at us? Did you think you could humiliate us by sending that nigra with the drum? You really think we're too stupid to see through your Yankee tricks? Look at you! May the Lord strike you down for wearing His sign when you're just another Yankee trespasser!"

"About the Negro—"

"How old are you?"

"Twenty-one, ma'am," I said, "but that's really not—"

"The sheer arrogance of a twenty-one year old boy pretending to be a reverend, banging at the door of a stranger. You know where the trouble all begins?"

"About the Negro—"

"It begins at childhood."

"Ma'am?"

"You people up North don't teach your children any social graces. By the time you grow up, you're savages."

With a regiment of Sherman's truculent, unwashed army roiling through the street, I was in no position to argue social graces. In the most deferential tone I could manage, I said, "Ma'am, I saw the Negro go around the side of your house. I would like to find him. I mean no trouble. I would just like to talk to him. I think he considers me a friend."

She clasped her hands, gripping them together, seriously trying to keep from striking out at me. "That arrogance again! You know nothing of these people. We are their friends. Right now, I'm seeing that he gets a meal. Did your army ever do as much? And do you truly want to help him? Send him back to the man who owns him! That would be the right thing to do!" When I made no reply, she went on, "Why am I wasting my time? You'll find the nigra in the kitchen, rear door, go on, go on, see your friend. Cleary! You get back inside!"

That last was to the boy, who had come silently to the top step of the porch. He stood stiffly, regarding the troops, a hand behind his back clutching a candlestick base, a heavy bit of pewter that would leave a bruise if hurled at someone. His mother had seen it before I did and she reached him in one stride, clasped him tightly and pulled him to the door. I glanced back as I descended the steps and our eyes met. Indignation was gone; fear was in its place.

At the rear, the door was opened by a short, stocky woman of middle years with deep black African coloring. She peered carefully around to make sure I was alone. When I told her I was Chaplain Brantley and I had come to see the man with the drum, she replied with startling ease and articulateness, "My name is Rosella. It's very thoughtful of you to visit him. Please come in."

The kitchen was large and shadowy, with windows covered by sheets of muslin, and lit only by a candle on a chopping-block table in the middle of the room. The old fellow was slowly pulling himself up from a stool by the table, a half-finished plate of food before him. Traces of cooking odors were in the air as well as the Negro odor which, I noted, no longer seemed strange to me.

"Sit down, Mose," I said. "You need some rest and you need to eat."

He looked at Rosella, who was bringing a stool for me.

She nodded at him and, after I had seated myself, he sat again, but made no move toward the food.

"William is a field man," she said, standing by him with a protective hand on his shoulder. "He's not accustomed to house ways."

"William? Not Mose? That was just a name they made up for you?"

He shrugged at that and said, "Willyam" haltingly, the first word I had heard him utter.

"You won't eat while I'm here, will you?" I asked. He looked away.

"The way he was raised, he can't bring himself to do that," Rosella said.

"All right, I'll go in a moment. I just want to know what he'll do now. The woman I spoke to said he should return to his owner. Does she know who that is? Would they take him back?"

William put a hand to his throat and Rosella said, "They would put a rope to him after whipping him near death. He's from a plantation, one of the worst kind. The missus here doesn't know. He can't stay. He has to go with the people following your army."

"The main part of the army is off fighting a battle, some place called Danner's Crossing."

"He'll get where he needs to be," Rosella said. "There are colored people around you don't see. They'll lead him when it gets dark. We've been preparing ever since we heard about Sherman coming this way."

The news gave me a bit of comfort and I wondered, given her obvious intelligence, if she was among those responsible for the preparing. I found myself looking from one to the other, contrasting William's slowness with her quickness. Over William's shoulder I saw the drum discarded in a corner and, behind it, a shelf filled with books. "Educated," flashed through my mind with surprise and, oddly, satisfaction. Rosella followed my gaze and I was certain she picked up my thoughts instantly.

"The South has its contradictions," I offered.

"As does the North, I'm sure," was all she answered.

With nothing more to say, and wanting William to finish his food, I rose to leave, praying with them first for God's grace. At the door, Rosella said, "Don't worry about William. Watch yourself now. You're a good man in a bad time. Watch yourself," she repeated.

We all want to be valued, don't we, my dear? Knowing God's love should be strength enough and yet the motherly warning of this colored woman, the first truly kind word I had heard since enlisting, brought a lightness to my step as I came outside.

There, my mood brightened still further. Despite Sherman's warning on the bluff, the church remained standing, bulky and shiny. Across the street, the park had been taken over by men at small cookfires. While missing planks from the bandstand told me where the wood came from, there was no other visible damage. The men relaxed quietly on the grass, talking and playing cards. In the nearby streets, the troops were equally peaceful, smoking and chatting while mounted officers watched closely. My respect for the major rose. He had his regiment in good discipline, preserving Sherman's often-violated edict against unprovoked destruction.

And with that, my love, this day ended. An officer pointed me to our new headquarters, the mill house on the far end of town, and it is from there that I write. More as soon as I can, with God's grace.

Your loving and devoted,
Ellis

CHAPTER THREE:

CLEARY

December 5, 1864

My Dearest Elaine,

I've placed myself under a sycamore behind the mill house with brown leaves around me, although they're not the cushion you'd find at home; the trees turn slowly here. The leaves that still cling to their limbs bring a pleasantly mottled sunlight onto the paper in my lap. It's a soft light, from a sun that still has some morning haze around it, in a sky of deep, unmarked blue, horizon to horizon. Save for a continual hammering sound (more about this shortly) I could picture you here beside me in one of those deliciously peaceful, loving moments...well, enough. I haven't learned yet how to balance the joy of imagining that we are together against the painful reality that we are not.

This mill house we commandeered is a cavernous place, with dim shafts of light from high, narrow windows, and I awoke this morning from a dream that I was back in a seminary classroom. That's not a complaint; the building, an old stone affair, is dry enough, although a bit musty, and so big it's become a temporary dormitory. Officers sleep on cots or bedrolls in rows wide enough for each of us to set up his table and chair. Normally we're in a field of one or two-man tents which, even though mere sheets of canvas, become homes, with the privacy and barriers the word 'home' connotes.

Here, we have a community instead and I took advantage of it. Most of the contingent was on duty in town but the rest, some fifteen men, were present. There are smaller congregations, I thought contentedly, standing up to announce a morning prayer time. The room quickly cleared of nine men who remembered various duties that needed their attention, leaving six, praise the Lord, who pulled their chairs into a half-circle before me. I noted that one of them, a tall and meticulously uniformed captain named Palmer, had been present at the incident with William.

Being the stranger in the gathering, as well as its instigator, I was obliged to offer some personal details and so I told of my years in seminary, our engagement (perhaps a bit too fervently but how can I be less than passionate about you?) and our plan to establish churches after the war in the new communities springing up beyond Missouri and Kansas.

Heavy clanking noises, metal hitting metal, began outside as I finished, but my listeners ignored it. They simply nodded at my words, courteously enough yet with no discernible warmth and no offer of biographical matter of their own, leaving me once again conscious of my low rank. We then prayed around—for the men now at Danner's Crossing, for the Union, for Sherman, Grant, Lincoln, families, friends, and even for the Confederate enemy—and I closed with a ten minute message on Paul's speech to the Athenians.

No one seemed to find significance in my choice of topic, a man standing alone against a crowd, except for Palmer, who gave me a waspish look when I finished. As the others offered their thanks and pulled their chairs back, he asked, "Ever seen a Sherman bow tie?" I knew what he meant: railroad tracks wrapped around a tree to make certain the enemy could never re-use them. I followed him outside.

After a moment to take in the scene, I learned how a train line could be demolished systematically, speedily, and merrily. Men armed with mallet, pickax and crowbar uprooted thirty-foot long iron rails. Other men swarmed in instantly to carry them into the flatland surrounding the mill house. There, they laid them across a wide, freshly dug trench that emitted puffs of smoke and popping cinders from a kindling-wood fire. The mallet-pickax-crowbar teams then pried out the heavy wooden ties beneath the rails and another waiting group immediately carted them off and eased them into the smoldering trench, under the rails, where they could fuel the fire.

Between the trench and the rail line was the source of the merriment: a group of three fiddlers, two banjoists and two guitarists, sawing and plucking away at a wordless old mountain melody called, and pardon the language, my dear, "Hell Broke Loose in Georgia." Men carrying rails or ties actually managed little hornpipe steps as they passed the musicians without breaking the speed and discipline of their work.

Palmer drew me along toward the trench, remarking in a condescending manner, "You did a little scouting with Uncle Billy the other night. Did you learn anything?"

I kept my tone respectful and serious. "I learned that he's a thoughtful and peaceful man who wages war because he must. I'd like to think we're all that way."

"Think what you will, many of us wage war because we've come to enjoy it. Did your years at seminary change you?"

"Of course."

"Then why wouldn't years of war change a man? Make him warlike. We're the product of what we do."

"You came to a prayer meeting this morning. You know we don't preach war."

"I came for the same reason Sherman likes to hear a sermon now and then. Curiosity."

I stopped and faced him. "Not about God, surely. Not about Scripture. About yourself? Like a swimmer in an undertow looking back at the shore: how far have I drifted?"

"You're very astute in some ways, Parson."

"No one drifts so far that God can't lead him back—"

He cut me off. "Please, no private sermons. Astute as you may be, you're out of tune with the world you live in. I could tell that you wanted to turn that old colored man loose the other morning, even take the matter up with your friend, Sherman." He smiled mockingly at "your friend."

I said nothing, taken aback that my intentions were so transparent.

"Sherman would have dismissed you instantly. You see those men?" He pointed to some rail-carriers doing a heel-and-toe as they passed the musicians. "They destroy and do a little dance at the same time. That's what the Negro episode was, a little dance."

"They didn't even know his name," I said. "They called him Mose. His name is William."

"That bothers you?"

"Couldn't they have left him that little bit of respect?"

"Did you take a good look at him? He was one of those field Negroes, barely smart enough to pluck a tobacco leaf."

We were now at the rim of the trench, where men lined up on each side waiting for the crosswise iron rails to glow red and soften at the center. "Hell Broke Loose in Georgia" came to an end and the music resumed with a melody I couldn't make out until a soldier on the opposite side of the trench threw me a grinning salute and I recognized that the little band was performing, in its own cracked way, "Amazing Grace." I turned to the musicians, who also grinned at me. I smiled and saluted them in return.

The captain leaned toward me to murmur, "You have

a measure of respect here because you preach dramatically and because you're honest. Your orderly has told them there's not a bit of pilfered property in your things and that you eat whatever the men eat, never asking him to scrounge up anything extra. Now take some advice from someone who knows this army well. Don't throw away the respect on foolish gestures."

I didn't answer. I simply stood there and gazed around, contemplating a fiery pit at my feet, a celestial blue sky above, God's own music at my back and Satan in the shape of an army captain whispering in my ear.

Could any seminary graduate ask for more?

We waited until a few of the rods had been bent around the nearest tree, then headed back to the mill house. Tomorrow is Sunday and I had started to mull over the message I would preach when Palmer abruptly asked, "Do you understand why I'm giving you advice?"

I weighed that for an instant, then replied, "I'd like to think it's for my benefit, to save me trouble, but I suspect it's only to save the army trouble."

"I'm not totally callous, Brantley. I wouldn't want to see you hurt. But it's clear to me that you're one of those pure-hearted jackasses who will somehow create a dangerous situation, for yourself and for others. And it will come on suddenly. You don't know war, so you don't know how quickly lives are taken or changed forever. That's why I look at you and see a problem in the making. Be very careful, Parson."

"I will be, Captain, in every way that's in my power."

Annoyance crossed his face. "Meaning you'll do what you wish and call it God's will." He marched off.

Lambert met me at the mill house door with word that Sherman's messenger had come by. I might have to preach in the field tomorrow, he reported. There had been only a few shots along the picket lines at Danner's Crossing, no real fighting yet, and if the situation held that way tomorrow I'd be sent for. Otherwise, I could preach to the troops here in town.

I regarded Lambert, wondering whether I should thank him for spreading the word that I'm an honest man, then decided it would embarrass us both.

"If I preach here, I would set up in that little park in town. Everything still peaceful? Discipline seemed to be good there last night."

"Well, none of the townfolk did anything stupid so that helped. Truth to tell, though, Parson, 'tain't so much discipline as space."

"Space?"

"Well, you see, we come in here with just the one regiment instead of three or four like usual, so each man's got a little bit of street that's his, some space to stretch his legs, visit with a chum, all that sort of thing. You put men shoulder against shoulder, all pressed in tight, well, you ever see too many dried beans in a pot?"

"Boils over," I said.

"Yeah, and soldiers won't boil over against their own, so it's the town that gets it. But this here town should get by, long as we move on soon."

And so my sweet Elaine, here I sit under the sycamore, musing again on how little I know of this war. Not discipline, but space. So obvious. Musing, also, on two warnings: a caring one yesterday from Rosella, a brusque one this morning from Palmer. I must pray for the strength to ignore them both when I'm called upon.

With love and devotion forever,
Ellis

December 6, 1864

My Darling Elaine,

The imprint on this paper bears a field hospital insignia, so I must tell you immediately that I am not injured. I am here tending to someone else. I will explain it all, warning you in advance that this day has been difficult. A surgeon here, who saw me writing and doubtless observed the grimness in my face, remarked, "Always send home cheerful letters, Chaplain. It doesn't help them to know the reality."

It made me suddenly aware that I'm helping myself by setting down the reality. To see it on paper is an exorcism of a sort, isn't it? I draw strength from God when I talk with Him, which should be enough for a cleric, yet I draw strength from you as well when I talk in these letters. Am I thus selfish? Am I inflicting pain on you? The surgeon, of course, knows nothing of your inner sturdiness, nor the harmony of our love, for each other and for Him, which commands complete truth on these pages. In all events, I'm simply incapable of anything else, my dearest, and so will resume the narrative here:

Sherman did indeed send for me this morning and I followed his sergeant along a series of roads and trails through the Georgia countryside for about an hour, coursing through dry meadowland and harvested peach orchards and plum thickets, paying close attention to the route at the sergeant's warning that I would probably have to make my way back alone. Everyone else would be moving on the Rebs by noon.

"Will this be a major battle?" I asked.

"Hard to say. We know Joe Wheeler's cavalry is there, maybe two regiments of horse. It's the foot soldiers where we have a puzzle. There's militia around, a home guard, we know that, but how many more men they gathered, maybe

33

some of Lee's army come south, no way to tell, so we're going heavy, in division strength I hear tell."

That was borne out after a few miles by the large numbers of men forming up in the meadows or visible in glimpses through the wooded patches, fidgety and loud, rifles slung over shoulders or cradled like loved ones to the bosom.

Another mile brought us to a little hollow, something of a natural theatre between gently rising slopes, blanketed with troops even more tightly packed than last Sunday's audience, understandable when men face combat.

Instead of ammunition boxes to stand on, this time I had a neatly constructed platform of fresh pine boards with three wide steps for an easy and dignified ascent, a welcome benefit of being headquarters chaplain. I tested the solid footing with a few little bounces as Sherman led his staff to the chairs in front.

General Slocum sat on one side of him and on the other, a general whose full gray beard rested in his lap, as did a large Bible, leather cover creased from heavy use: Oliver Otis Howard, "Old Prayer Book" himself, come over from his Army of the Tennessee to be with Sherman for this battle.

I was about to start when Sherman abruptly stood and strode to the platform. "Chaplain," he said, "you know these men are moving into battle right after this?"

I tapped my Bible. "First Chronicles, Chapter Five. The sons of Reuben and their allies go to war against the Hagarites and their allies."

He nodded and returned to his seat, leaving me a bit exasperated. Did he really think I might preach a sermon about charity and love in this situation? Was it our conversation on the bluff? Had I sounded overly pacifist? Had he heard about my concern for William? Whatever the case, I had crafted a warlike message and, spurred now by his question, turned it into an oration.

I began by speaking directly to the troops, ignoring the formalities of introducing myself or acknowledging that high-ranking officers were present.

"Forty-four thousand, seven hundred sixty men once went into battle," I announced. I pointed to the Bible for authentication and continued, "Forty-four thousand seven hundred sixty righteous men, men who believed the word of God, men who called upon His divine help."

I waited until I was sure they had absorbed the number and "righteous" and identified themselves with both, then spent about ten minutes explaining the historic setting of First Chronicles, invoking the familiar names of David and Saul and extolling their episodes of passionate service to the Lord. I moved on to the less frequently told tale of the sons of Reuben for another five minutes, tracing their lineage and steadfast faith, and then, stepping to the very edge of the platform, I dwelt on the idolatry and wicked transgressions of the neighboring Hagarites and their allies.

In a steadily rising voice, I cited what Psalm Eighty-three said about them: "Keep not thou silent, O God... thine enemies make a tumult and they that hate thee have lifted up the head...they have taken crafty counsel against thy people...they have said, come and let us cut them off from being a nation." I lingered over that for a moment here in this secessionist state of Georgia, then concluded the verse, "That the name of Israel may be no more in remembrance."

I raised my arms to heaven at that point like a temple priest and, applying my seminary knowledge of Hebrew and the most thunderous voice I could summon, cried out in the ancient language for retribution. The words were strange but the meaning was unmistakable and there were cries of "Amen" from all around, even the front row.

Going back to the words of First Chronicles about the Reubenite army, I said, "They were valiant men," and, sweeping the open Bible over them as if in benediction, repeated, "valiant men," then continued, cradling each phrase, "men able to bear buckler and sword and to shoot with bow.....and skillful in war."

I could see men unthinkingly touch their cartridge packs, bayonets and rifles as if they were buckler, sword and bow, while the words "skillful in war" brought heads high and, through the alchemy of pride, the ranks seemed to expand in place.

You know the final verses of the passage, my dear: the humbling of the Hagarites on the field and "the capture of their cattle: of camels, fifty thousand, and of their sheep, two hundred fifty thousand, and of asses two thousand, and of men an hundred thousand."

Then I said to this army of foragers, "Now I have never seen a camel in Georgia, have you?"

The scattered "No's" came and I continued, "Well, if there is one, this is the only army in history that can track it, find it, bring it in and cook it up into the world's finest camel fricassee."

There was a pause that alarmed me. Had I crossed some unknown line of behavior for chaplains? Then the men erupted into laughter that filled the hollow and didn't lessen until I steepled my hands and began to pray, asking for God's hand of protection for all on the field of battle, carefully not specifying one side or the other, although this was largely lost. The men had been roused and a mixture of chatter and gleeful elbowing underlay my words.

General Howard came to me, grasped my shoulder

and proclaimed that I was an inspired preacher and, despite my youth, Sherman had made a fine choice in asking me to speak. That made me glance at Sherman, who sat in his camp chair and contemplated me with eyes half closed and thin lips pursed, an expression that vanished as he saw me watching. I recognized it, though: sadness, of all things. I had delivered the sermon he wanted, the men were primed to face the enemy, his chief subordinate had publicly praised me and yet this unexpectedly deep man of war was saddened. You'll understand, Elaine, that he rose in my estimation and Captain Palmer, who thought this general enjoyed war, seemed less of a sage to me.

All of it—the reaction of the men to the sermon, Howard's compliments, Sherman's attitude—left me satisfied riding back to Hillardville and I wish the day had ended there. As I emerged from the shadows of a peach orchard into clear meadow, I saw a column of smoke, thin, but dark and dense, rising from the direction of the town.

I raced ahead, watching the sky, hopeful as the column remained the same. Just one building, I thought, not the whole town, and probably not the church. The massive old building would produce thick billows, not a column. As I neared the main thoroughfare, I saw that I was correct. The smoke had one source, a house afire somewhere in the street.

The town itself, however, took me a long, stunned moment to comprehend. In place of the sparsely patrolled and quiet avenue I had left was a violent scene of soldiers swarming the road in closely packed gangs, shoving and pushing, yelling, swearing and flourishing household contraband: pots, lamps, paintings, hams, loaves of bread, books whose pages were being torn and scattered like confetti, a piano bench, wine bottles—an empty one struck my horse's flank and he almost threw me until I steadied the poor beast down—blankets, torn draperies, shoes and boots, and garments belonging to men, women and children, with intimate feminine items provoking the most appalling guffaws and offensive language.

I pushed on, wiping away tears of rage, of shock, of despair, passing houses with doors torn off the hinges, windows shattered, soldiers (can I still call this ransacking mob soldiers?) wrestling and punching each other as those trying to get in through a door or window collided with those trying to get out with their spoils.

In the midst of a trampled front garden, a cavalry officer slumped sidesaddle, leaning on his horse's neck as casually as one would recline on a divan. I composed myself and worked my way to his side. He sat up straight until he could make out that I was a chaplain, not a senior officer, and slumped over again. He was himself a lieutenant, my age or younger.

"No place for a man of God, brother," he said, slurring words enough to reveal he was mildly drunk, although coherent.

"What happened to the regiment that was here this morning?" I asked. "Who's here now?"

"Uncle Billy called your regiment up to join his rear guard and sent us over from the Tennessee to be his reserve."

"Looks like a lot more than one regiment."

"Well, sure, Parson," he said. "We're a brigade, what you need for reserve in a major battle. You must be new to all this. You hungry? Plenty of food here, brandy, too." He pointed at the house behind him. "I'm guarding it," he chuckled.

Ignoring that, I said, "The town was peaceful when I left this morning."

"Peaceful when we got here, too. Then some damn

fool Rebel boy fired a shot at a soldier, dumbest thing ever, set everybody off—hey, you want to stay out of the street, Parson!" he shouted at my back as I pushed into the mob again, making my way toward the other end, thinking of Lambert's words about men needing space—a brigade meant three regiments packed together instead of just the one—and thinking of Cleary, the foolhardy boy with the candlestick base, and his angry, fearful mother, and Rosella.

The closer I came, prying my way through sweating grinning faces, blindly grinning back to avert any quarrels, the more apparent it became that the house on fire was the house I had visited and the more certain grew my conviction that the "damn fool Rebel boy" was Cleary, lying dead.

I turned out to be partly right. It was indeed Cleary, but he was still alive, stretched out on the lawn of the church while across the avenue his house spouted flames from every window. Only the space between houses in this wealthy part of Hillardville kept the blaze confined, with cinders and sparks landing on the grass where a few neighbors, white women and some female slaves armed with water buckets, quenched them quickly.

What truly alarmed me was the clustered mass of soldiers before the house, fascinated by the flames, some silently entranced, others whooping as sudden spurts of fire leaped from a window or through the roof. Would this be enough to satiate them? Would they need more after the inevitable collapse of this building?

At least they were paying no mind to Cleary, who lay shuddering and crying, his mother kneeling by him, stroking his hair and whispering to him. The boy's right leg was twisted, obviously broken. He was holding his stomach tightly with both hands and his face was bruised red and raw, evidence of a beating that undoubtedly left many more wounds than the visible ones.

His mother started wildly when I dismounted, then scuttled on hands and knees into a shell over the boy's body.

"I won't hurt him. I'm the chaplain, Ellis Brantley. We met two days ago. He needs to go to the field hospital."

She stayed rigid, not looking at me, and murmured, "Rosella said that." Then she shook her head and added, "Yankee doctors."

"Doctors are sworn to help," I assured her, not really certain of the attitude we'd find, wondering simultaneously where the hospital was and how I could transport Cleary. There was no way to position him on my horse, let alone ride with him through this mob.

With no officer in sight here, I prepared to return to the mildly drunken lieutenant to ask the hospital location and then try the improbable task of enlisting his help in getting a wagon. I had my foot in the stirrup when a donkey cart jounced around from the rear of the church, a small Negro boy at the reins, Rosella beside him. Showing no surprise at finding me here, she said to the boy, "I won't need you now, the preacher will help us." She didn't bother to look at me for confirmation. The boy did look, with an expression that told me I was an angel direct from heaven, before he jumped down and disappeared.

I lifted the boy while Rosella held his leg steady and together we managed to lay him in a carpet of grass and straw that had been arranged with foresight over the rough boards. The boy's mother clambered in beside him, pillowing his head and Rosella joined them while I quietly tied my horse to the back of the cart, then climbed onto a few nailed-together planks that formed a seat of sorts.

"Go behind the church, the way I came," Rosella whispered, relieving my deep anxiety about trying to force a way through the raging streets. We had instinctively been quiet to avoid attention, even Cleary, but at the first jolt of the little cart he screamed and though his mother immediately cut it off with a hand over his mouth, a handful of men drifted over from the perimeter of the mob.

They gazed wordlessly at us, resentment mingling in their expressions with uncertainty at the sight of my uniform, until a thin and shaggy-headed fellow, the drunkest or boldest of the lot, leaned over the cart with fists upraised. The others followed his lead, gathering around menacingly, with the words, "Stinkin' Reb" and "Nigra trash" coming hoarsely from one of them.

Before I could gather breath to announce I was General Sherman's chaplain and a noose awaited the man who touched any one in this cart, Cleary's mother had raised herself to her knees. Her dress was torn, her hair unpinned, her face dirty with soot and ashes, and the arms she held over her child were a thin and trembling shield. Altogether, she was as tired and defenseless a sight as one might wish to see, looking at the hostile group before her, each man in turn.

It arrested them for a moment, enough time for me to pat the donkey into motion. One of the rioters took a few steps alongside, spitting out at the woman, "We see that boy again, we'll kill him," while the shaggy one came to my side and muttered, "You like Rebs and monkey women too much. We'll remember you, Parson."

Once we rounded the side of the church, Cleary's mother sagged back beside him and Rosella leaned over to embrace them, as though mother to both, then sat up to direct me through a field behind the building, finding a path that was little more than a streak of matted grass I never would have seen.

It occurred to me I didn't know the family name of the people I was helping and I asked Rosella.

"DeRoche," she told me. "Anita DeRoche. She's Irish, that's how Cleary got his name, and he's Swiss, Albert DeRoche, a colonel with Stuart's cavalry. One of them is noisy, one of them is quiet, and I won't tell you which is which, just that they're perfectly suited, a couple that shouldn't be apart."

She was silent a moment, then went on to tell me that Cleary knew about a pistol in the house, a weapon his father left behind in the event his mother had to defend herself in some desperate circumstance. The boy went to the porch, cursed at the soldiers and fired a shot. Although it hit nobody, it gave them a reason to erupt.

"They would have found a reason in any—" I started, then swiveled around at a spate of yelling with a piercing and excited new tone to it. Men were now swarming around the church, many with torches, and a star-shaped patch of flame appeared like a stigmata on the white walls where lamp oil had been flung. I stood up as it spread and multiplied, a mad impulse to go back, to attempt to stop it, actually going through my head. I must have been hollering, for Rosella was saying, "Shush now, Reverend, shush, only wood and nails, a building's only wood and nails."

I sat down, looking into the cart, intending to apologize—they certainly needed no outburst from me after all they had endured—but Cleary was asleep or unconscious with his mother clasping him, unmindful of anything else.

Rosella moved back with them and I saw that her planning had included two pails of water and some cloths tucked against the side of the cart. She began to bathe their faces, again like a mother to both, and I glimpsed why Rosella might help slaves like William to go north but would not go herself.

"Contradictions," I said.

"South and North," she agreed, as she had done in the kitchen.

When we reached a wide and well-worn road she sat up and told me to turn right and keep on going. "You'll have no trouble finding the hospital when you're close. Just follow the smell."

"You talk as though you're leaving us," I said with obvious uneasiness.

"Where you takin' this nigra monkey woman, Parson?" she rasped, in perfect imitation of the soldier who had threatened me.

"All right, your presence could slow us down," I conceded, reining in the donkey.

"And I have to go to the neighbors and arrange living quarters for us, presuming Cleary lives and the neighbors still have houses." As she climbed off, she said, "The Lord knows each and every man who's burning that church, Reverend, each and every one, and He will judge them. Go quickly now."

The donkey balked, looking after Rosella when I tried to turn, but she walked purposefully, steady as a much younger woman, with no looking back, and the donkey settled in, moving us at a far better pace on this new road.

The hospital turned out to be a commandeered farmhouse flanked by a row of Sibley tents, spacious wigwam-like structures tethered into one unit. The smell had guided me as Rosella predicted but it came only in occasional drifts, not the steady stench I had feared. The reason became clear—thankfully so—as we rattled up to the farmhouse. The battle of Danner's Crossing had evidently not produced any casualties yet and the only patients would be some men who were ill, not wounded. Doctors, nurses and medical orderlies lounged outside on the farmhouse steps or on the grass, although their ease was belied by the array of stretchers and straps and a wheeled table of bandage rolls within quick reach.

We were surrounded instantly, Cleary was moved gently but swiftly to a stretcher, no comments or questions about a Rebel boy were uttered and a nurse put comforting arms around Mrs. DeRoche and led her away to the women's quarters when she tried to follow the stretcher into the house.

It was dusk by now, growing too dark for me to find my way back safely, and I gratefully accepted an orderly's suggestion to have dinner here and spend the night. I might be in some difficulty tomorrow for not returning immediately to Slocum's command, my official post, but will face up to that when, and if, necessary.

Meanwhile, I have the chance to write to you, my dearest, and to check on Cleary and Anita DeRoche in the morning. I'm content that they're in caring hands. When the orderly brought me stationery, I said, "You treat people as patients here, not Yanks or Rebs, don't you?"

"Long as your officers ain't around, meaning no disrespect, sir," he replied.

And with that I come to the end of this letter, my dearest, that church still burning in my memory. I know He will judge the guilty ones, as Rosella said, and the man of earthly sense inside me says I'm fortunate I was removed by events before I could try to be heroic, alone against a maddened mob. Yet the sight of flame consuming that pristine white wall...wood and nails, wood and nails, I know.

I must pray now.

Your loving and devoted,
Ellis

CHAPTER FOUR:
DANNER'S CROSSING

December 7, 1864

My Dearest Elaine,

I was able to lead a worship service in the hospital this morning and everyone seemed grateful. They have no chaplain of their own and there is nothing like injury or ill health to motivate faith. It's not only the patients. It extends to the physicians and the staff since they spend their time in such close proximity to suffering.

More of the suffering springs from disease than from shot or shell, a fact we used to read about in the newspapers. The reports were always in remote corners of the publication—battles are so much more stimulating to read about—but listening this morning to a nurse and her patient, a colonel feverish with malaria, educated me in the anguish of those struck down by sickness.

We were at the colonel's bedside, where I prayed for his recovery. He whispered, "Miracle," in response. The nurse explained that recovery was not anyone's expectation with malaria and the colonel's goal was to tolerate this attack, then return to his unit and perform his duties until the next attack put him back in bed. Knowing the remainder of his life would follow this pattern, the colonel had turned down a medical discharge to delay, as long as possible, going home to burden his wife and children.

He raised a hand in agreement, sipping some cold coffee from a cup held by the nurse, but as she was telling him she was sure his family would welcome him home and be eager to help him, he abruptly knocked the cup to the floor and called loudly and irrationally, "Measles ward, at once! Measles ward!"

His forehead erupted in perspiration and he began a rambling history of the men who died of measles in his command, calling out names and, with details I will spare you, the ravages of the disease, and then going on to those hit by dysentery, by typhoid, and by his own affliction. His voice ranged from whispers to shouts, and he was obviously going through a delirium, yet the truth of his account came through, a despairing tale of a silent, invincible enemy shredding his regiment, told with immense sorrow for the fallen and no pity for himself.

His eyes closed then and he became quiet, the effect of laudanum in the coffee, the nurse told me. The colonel, she went on, was a Minnesotan, had fought with Grant the length of the Mississippi and now with Sherman through Tennessee and Georgia, giving him three years and two thousand miles of sending more men to hospital than into battle.

I remarked that this hospital was almost empty; there were no more than a dozen beds occupied.

"We're getting some relief," she answered, "finally." She was a woman of forty-five, I estimated, and I wondered how many years and how many miles of this war she had endured.

"Sherman's armies are the survivors," she continued, "the toughest ones. Those who were physically unfit to begin with—there were no real standards for enlisting, you know—and those who were vulnerable to sickness, they're all weeded out now. From here to Virginia, your Uncle Billy is riding sixty thousand panthers."

And a fair share of hyenas, I muttered to myself. We had reached Cleary's bedside, bringing yesterday sharply to mind, so forgive the un-Christian bitterness, my dear. You know I pray for the troops, and most fervently for the worst sinners among them.

Cleary's leg was in a splint that ran from ankle to thigh and his head was wrapped in bandages. The splint was a good sign, the nurse said. It meant we had arrived before gangrene could set in. The leg would heal and he could be released today. The other injuries, as bloody as they had seemed, were minor and the resiliency of youth would see them fade quickly.

None of this was reflected in Cleary's face. The sullen look I had seen through the window of his house was even darker now. Without looking at me, he said, "Thank you, Reverend Brantley," obviously instructed by his mother.

She showed some color in her face this morning. Her hair was fixed and a red shawl borrowed from the nurses covered her torn dress. She sat erect, deliberately composed, trying to be as stately here as she would be in her own drawing room. Her voice was strong and certain once more.

"Thank you, Reverend Brantley. You performed a very brave deed in support of people who are your enemies, a truly Christian act. I said some offensive things to you the other day and I retract them and apologize for them."

Only the words were correct. The tone was formal, overly so, and simply reflected her obeisance to the "social graces" she had hurled at me on the porch. The difference between her attitude and Cleary's, I saw, was a matter of manners, nothing more.

I was undisturbed by it. Expectations of mortal gratitude were not my motive last night and I replied simply, "It was a time of high emotional stress, Mrs. DeRoche. Apologies are accepted, although certainly not necessary. Tell me, what will you do now?"

"Return to Hillardville. Rosella's grandson—the boy you saw last night—was here earlier. The road is clear, the troops are gone and our neighbors are on the way to take us to their home. You need not worry about us any longer."

After praying at the bedside, devoting much of it to a plea for Cleary's healing, with my voice pitched at him, I departed, stopping long enough to set down these events, partially to fill my need to stay in contact with you, my dear, and partially to contemplate on paper, out of perverseness, the people I have met so far who genuinely consider me a friend. There's Rosella, William, possibly Lambert, who at least thinks I'm honest, and that's about the extent of it.

So with that disposed of (and how I love you for allowing me such childish lapses!) I will head for Danner's Crossing.

Your devoted and so frequently undeserving,
Ellis

December 8, 1864

My Darling Elaine,

The calendar tells me it's the second week of December and I'm tempted to ask about the snow at home, about the signs of Christmas that must be appearing (are there paper angels yet on the schoolhouse windows?) but you would guess that I'm simply delaying my account of today's happenings and you would be right. Stop for a moment here and pray for resilience because this will be difficult reading.

About two hours north of the hospital I saw a soldier in a gray Rebel coat stumbling through thin clumps of grass some fifty yards from me, then falling and crawling toward a crumbling stone fence, looking back at me every few seconds, trying to reach some cover.

Riding toward him, I held my hand out, fingers spread in a sign of peace. He still kept crawling until I wheeled around in front of him, dismounted and looked into the face of a mere boy, afraid for a bewildering second that Cleary had somehow gotten here. As I knelt before him, I could see he was older than Cleary but not by much, a couple of years perhaps, downy-cheeked beneath blotches of blood, staring at me in panic.

"No, no," I said, "I'm a chaplain, I will not hurt you. Can you ride if I help you up?" I reached for him and his arms and legs gave way under him. He collapsed to one side, then rolled on his back, revealing a wound in his stomach that sickened me. More description than that you do not need. I looked around wildly at the empty fields and untraveled road, then simply put his head in my lap. I lifted a tag from around his neck: Jonathan Raymond, Georgia Home Guard, Dawson.

"Jonathan," I said without preamble, suspecting I had little time, "do you know and love our Lord Jesus Christ?"

There was no speech in him, only gasping little breaths but he heard me and, to my joy, he managed to mouth, "Yes." He reached a shaky hand out, searching. I clasped it, told him that a home in glory surely awaited him and, just to keep a caring voice in his ear, began to talk, relating the tale of Elijah on the mountainside seeking the word of the Lord, finding it not in wind or fire or earthquake, but in a gentle whisper, and the boy's face grew more and more peaceful, the painful breaths less and less frequent.

I continued with the majestic passage from Mattthew, "When the Son of man shall come in his glory and all the holy angels with him, then shall He sit upon the throne of his glory; and before him shall be gathered all nations." By the time I reached the words, "Come, ye blessed of my Father, inherit the kingdom prepared for you," the boy was already in that kingdom.

After some more time in prayer—I was standing then, head bowed over the youth, not even conscious that I had gotten to my feet—a wagon approached from the north, the direction of Danner's Crossing. I mounted and rode over quickly as two Union soldiers climbed out, hauling a trundle cart from the wagon bed while a third man, a white-bearded sergeant, stayed at the reins.

"They'll see to the boy," he said. "You're Reverend Brantley, the chaplain? They been looking for you. Lots of burials to attend to." He gestured to the north and to the back of the wagon where I made out the shapes of two bodies, maybe three, under a layer of burlap sacking.

I started to spur the horse and then, realizing that the body in the field was too far away for features to be seen, I turned and asked, "How did you know it was a boy?"

"You'll see as you go north. They're all boys, just young boys. God'amighty, Reverend!" he cried out suddenly. "Wickedest thing I ever saw, the chickens they lined up to fight grown men! All boys, except a few old fellows who could hardly limp across a field."

"I don't understand."

"Well, Reverend, there's a militia base near here—"

"Yes, I heard that," I broke in. "I thought it meant men with some training, and there was cavalry, and Lee was supposed to send troops—"

"Well, there was cavalry all right, rounding up these school boys, that's all this militia had, and a few men, hauled out of their rocking chairs, it looked like, and forcing them into formation and sending them to meet the toughest and meanest army in creation—just look at us! You know what we are, and the Rebs sure know what we are. They run like jackrabbits from a real battle. And as for Lee's troops, that was just wild talk, I mean the kind of surprise Uncle Billy and his generals have to look out for, like happened at Shiloh, but just wild talk here."

"What was the purpose then?"

"The purpose? Maybe to check our locations though for sure we're not hiding, maybe to see if we're getting fat and sloppy after swallowing Atlanta, maybe to tie us down while they raided the rear looking for supply lines which they should know darn well by now we don't have. You look for some sense to this, Reverend, you won't find it." He paused and stared at my lapel cross.

"Don't let this shake your trust in the Lord, Sergeant. Can you promise me that?"

He pointed up the road. "Ten, eleven miles, you'll see the burying ground." He avoided my eyes by gazing into the field, where the soldiers were easing the body into the cart.

"Psalm Thirty-seven," I said. "Please find a Bible and a quiet place to read it. Psalm Thirty-seven," I repeated and turned north again.

Other body-collecting crews were out on their grim harvest and I passed one cart heading south, toward the hospital, holding two boys, one lying flat, while the other sat, eyes glazed, patting his comrade's head mechanically.

A mile or so farther, a handsome black chaise approached, carrying two women, one of middle years, the other in her late teen years, both elegantly dressed, both slumping wearily and, unlike Anita DeRoche, making no pretense of being anything but exhausted and forlorn.

"Good day, sir," said the older. "Have you seen any Confederate casualties?"

"Yes, behind me there are two wounded in one cart and,

I'm grieved to say, three or four dead in another. You're seeking boys from close by? Those you know?"

"To give them a proper burial, yes."

"Is Dawson near here? Would you know a boy named Jonathan Raymond?"

"No. Dawson's a hundred miles away."

The younger one suddenly leaned halfway out of the chaise. "How do you know this boy was from Dawson? How do you know his name? Did you have anything to do with murdering him?"

"I'm a chaplain. I have no weapons. I found Jonathan wounded and tried to comfort him. I can tell you he was a believer and he's with our Lord now."

She sat back and buried her head in her hands.

"There's a burial ground to the north," I told the other woman. "I'm going there if you wish to follow me."

"Thank you. We've been there." She snapped the reins and they moved on.

A few more miles and a meadow opened on my right where groups of Negroes with carts were scouring the wooded borders for bodies. The largest part of the collecting and stacking had already been done. The far end of the meadow displayed dark and shapeless mounds many yards across and shoulder high in some places. Other Negroes with shovels waited at the treeline while troops stood around and Sherman—no mistaking the rumpled uniform and tired angle of the head—walked among the mounds. An officer with him pointed to me and the general waved me to his side.

"Had your baptism, didn't you," he remarked calmly as I dismounted, ignoring my salute and pointing at the front of my uniform. I discovered smears of blood, knees to chest. "Any of that your own?"

"No, sir."

"Ministering to the wounded?"

"One dying boy."

"One dying boy," he repeated. He paused as if he had some advice to add, then said, "Well, Palmer will take you where you're needed," and resumed his walking.

I hadn't noticed it was Captain Palmer with him. The immaculate officer of two days ago was now as rumpled as the general, with black stains that looked like locomotive soot on his clothes. He saw me looking and explained, "Artillery. Stand near the field pieces and they kick up a shower of dirt and oil." He brushed at his uncombed hair and added with disdain, "I've completed your combat education now, Chaplain."

My patience was gone, of course, after the strain of the morning. Please forgive me, my dear.

"You think being sarcastic with me is an answer for this? You said I would be a problem, Captain, so please tell me if I'm the problem here. Did I send these boys to fight? Did I tear them apart with rifle shot and cannon ball? Is there still enjoyment for you in this war? Do you think the general is enjoying it?"

The answer, of sorts, came from the general himself. My voice had been louder than I knew.

"Gentlemen," said Sherman.

We turned. A passing ray of afternoon sunlight brightened his hair, which you may know from newspaper descriptions is a dusky red, making him look either angelic or demonic for the moment, take it as you will.

"Press on," he said evenly.

Palmer and I saluted and he led me wordlessly to a glade just inside the first stand of pines. The Negro workers had started to dig the trenches that would become common gravesites. One of them was reserved for Union soldiers. The youthful attackers, though hopelessly outgunned, did manage to get off some rounds that landed. Nineteen other trenches were dug over the course of the afternoon, dug and filled with the blanket-covered bodies of the Rebel boys, some fifteen or twenty in each grave. The bodies seemed to become larger and heavier with the coming of twilight.

The scene grew more and more crowded as officers from Sherman's command came by and took up places on both sides of each trench. Torches were lit, making the scene yet more eerie and somber. Sherman had left during the digging, then returned for the funeral service, standing opposite me, face immobile. General Howard joined him, holding his ever-present leather Bible, silently but openly weeping. It was Howard's command that had seen the action, Howard's troops that had won this victory.

Yet neither general interested me as much as Palmer. I saw him through the leaping shadows thrown by the torches, standing at the parade rest position, legs apart, spine erect, shoulders back, jaw set, every inch the picture of military self-control under pressure.

Why then was I reminded of words you spoke to me before my first public sermon? "Don't stand up there like Caesar reviewing his legions. Everyone knows you're uncertain and vulnerable."

If that makes no sense, put it down to extreme fatigue. I'm writing in a comfortable tent that Lambert has set up for me and, without even trying to fight off any guilt about the luxury, I will sleep now. In the morning, when I am fresher, I will compose a letter to the Raymond family of Dawson, Georgia.

I pray I have not burdened you too much.

Your devoted and loving,
Ellis

CHAPTER FIVE:
DOROTHEA

December 14, 1864

My Sweet Elaine,

I'm lifted by two shafts of light in all the spiritual darkness that followed Danner's Crossing but first, let me tell of the army's difficult path this last week.

When we moved on, it was to the southeast, into Georgia swamp country where the roads became soft and boggy. The tidal streams, once placid and easy to bridge, were suddenly deeper and swifter and they seemed to be everywhere. At least once a day, sometimes twice, we inched along pontoon bridges that bounced like corks in the black-water currents. Once across, the wagons struggled and floundered in the mud while the long, swaggering strides of the foot soldiers were now reduced to slogging, cursing steps.

Setting up a tent for the night was hardly worth the muck it produced and nothing unnecessary was unpacked, including writing implements. Indeed, there was not even a way out for mail-carrying vehicles. The oppressive geography of the place was compounded here by Confederate forces, thicker than before, making an effort to harass us with sudden skirmishes, obliging us to stay unencumbered and ready to move instantly.

Sherman's goal is Savannah, connecting us with the ocean. The Union fleet is standing offshore and, once the city is captive, ships will bring in fresh supplies of weapons and ammunition and, especially important right now, food. The swamp country was not the easy foraging terrain we had left, with its farms full of livestock and grain. We were often down to one meal a day, and that a handful of corn or beans and hardtack.

Yet, despite all the obstacles of mud and hunger and Rebel forces, this relentless army has ground down the resistance and is now within a dozen miles of the city, on dryer ground, where we have settled peacefully and I am able to write once more.

The first shaft of light was a rise in attendance at Sunday services and at morning prayer meetings. The mud and the Rebel skirmishers, rather than becoming obstacles to worship, seemed to become incentives. Men crammed themselves into the miry clearings we found for Sunday mornings, overflowing beyond sight into the moss and cypress groves, standing up without complaint (impossible to sit in the mud) and bearing expressions almost triumphant at being there. The morning meetings for officers, previously attended by some half-a-dozen, now drew three and four times that number, all but one asking questions, sharing favorite verses and recalling tales of church back home with a quietly eager attitude. Palmer was the one exception, always present but taciturn and unreadable. That, at least, was an improvement over his usual sardonic manner.

The other shaft of light was provided by two sergeants, identical twins, large, unshaven and muscular, either one of them intimidating on sight in the way of Sherman's older veterans and, taken together, enough to make me tighten inside as they walked swiftly towards me.

After casual salutes all around—I had learned the indifferent touch of hand-to-cap that passes for military greeting here—they regarded me for a moment. With dress as casual as saluting in this army, I was conscious of the patched and wrinkled garb of my visitors compared to my clean uniform, polished brass and freshly shined boots, all courtesy of Lambert this morning. To my surprise, a glance of approval darted between them.

"I'm Samuel Ward, Parson," said one of them, "and this is my brother, Silas." Silas pointed to a wide scar on his brow as an aid to me in telling them apart.

"Ellis Brantley, headquarters chaplain. How can I help you?"

"They say, well, to speak plain, the talk around is that you're real quick to help people."

"Someone who might stretch himself a bit," put in Silas.

"Yeah, stretch himself a bit if you saw someone in a desperate way."

What they implied, of course, is that I was daring enough to bend or break regulations for the right cause, a reputation that came as no surprise to me after Palmer's warnings, and a reputation I accepted, I confess it, with a touch of self-congratulation. I'll pause while you once again shake your head and say, "Ellis, Ellis, Ellis."

I kept my face expressionless and asked, "Who? And how desperate?"

"'Bout ten miles back, where the marshes start firming up, there's a family, not the usual kind—"

"Girl, maybe fifteen," Silas picked up, "caring for her brother and sister, real little ones, nobody to help them."

"They can't stay where they are. You'll see why if you come with us," Samuel continued.

"You have food and supplies for them?"

"There's a cart ready, just down the road."

"Then why do you need me?"

"Parson, we can look in a mirror. Were you a girl, would you go with us?"

The trail they chose curved to the southwest, retracing ground the army had traveled last week.

Samuel rode at my side with Silas behind us driving a cart obviously spirited from some nearby farm. The sides were battered and gray with wood mold but the wheels and tongue were new.

"You were busy," I remarked, "gathering food, fixing this cart. This errand is important to you, isn't it?"

"Some friends in the engineers did the cart," was all the answer he gave. Then, about a quarter mile on, he turned to me and said, almost angrily, "Gotta give something back. Five hundred miles of taking, gotta give something back."

Thank you, Lord, I thought, thank you for the good men among the ravagers.

"How did you find them?" I asked.

"Went looking for them."

I gave him a minute, then said, "That's all you want to tell me?"

"It's all I want to tell you but I'm obliged to give you the rest, you coming out to help us. It don't say much about this army. Lots of good men, but some others—you seen them get wild?"

"I was at Hillardville."

He nodded. "Two men—always been trouble, these two—got hold of some mash, got liquored up, started talking about this farm they'd come to. Farmer away fighting, woman there with a good-looking daughter and two little ones. Started laughing and bragging about what they done to the woman. I'm talking wickedness here, Preacher, worst you can do to a woman. We found her body, buried her in a family gravesite up on a little hill. But the daughter got away with the little ones, sneaked into the root cellar and out through a tunnel they dug just for a situation like this. Silas and me, we went looking for them this morning. Can't survive this countryside all on your own, surely not with children to care for."

"But what about those men?"

"Them, yeah, well, they started cursing because they lost the daughter and going on about what they could have done with her and the rest of us put a stop to it. No point to you repeating that, though."

He was right; nobody would bring charges against men who dispensed justice to a rapist. It's the unpardonable crime, even among the worst of the looters and rioters.

"We found the children this morning," Samuel said, "but they were frightened near death of us, and the girl has a pistol. She threatened to shoot the little ones and herself if we came any closer. It's an old Uhlinger pocket piece, probably wouldn't even fire but we couldn't be sure. That's why we sought you out."

"After you bring them some food, then what?"

"Find a family between here and Savannah that would take them in. Or in Savannah, maybe a big church, big enough to organize help for people. Try to get a letter to their father. Could be we'd call on you again there, you know, talk preacher to preacher with their minister."

"All right," I agreed, welcoming the chance to meet a Southern clergyman, whatever the reason.

Another five miles and we turned into a trail made passable only by rocks and tree roots just below the mud. Overhanging vines and swamp oak turned it dark and cold. The trail ended at a shelter for those needy enough to hunt snakes and turtles in this mudscape, a mean little shack of roughly cut logs with a roof of wagon canvas.

When we dismounted, Silas came to me with a cloth and began to rub the grime of the road from my boots and my insignia, buffing the bits of brass, while Samuel patted dust and mud spots from my uniform. Silas then produced a blue lacy sweater, a rag doll and a toy wooden horse from the cart and put them in my hand.

"Both of us have wives and children back home," Samuel said. "Learned a bit. Also, the sight of these things could keep the girl from taking a shot at you."

"What?"

"Just fall on the floor should she she point it at you. If that old thing does go off, the recoil will put the round in the ceiling most likely."

I walked toward the door, accepting the casual attitude veteran soldiers have toward firearms and simultaneously irritated at the potential indignity of being shot by a backwoods girl on a muddy trail instead of on a battlefield.

Only when I reached the shack did I consider the real possibility of taking a bullet. The door was nothing but a few thin boards hinged by bits of rope and a shot might tear right through it, even from a pocket piece. With a dour glance back at Samuel and Silas, I knocked. A murmur from inside that I couldn't make out was the only response. After a moment I slowly pulled the door open, standing aside, tensed for the crack of a pistol.

My fears were needless. The girl was sprawled asleep on the dirt floor with the pistol by her hand. I recognized the outspread arms and and legs as signs of exhaustion. Huddled in a corner were two children—a girl of about five and a boy of perhaps three—clinging to each other, the girl singing quietly to the boy, the murmuring I heard.

I tossed the pistol out the door as a signal to Samuel and Silas, put the toys on the floor, draped the sweater on the sleeping form, then sat by her side. I slipped the Bible from my coat and said as softly as I could, "Let all bitterness, and wrath, and anger, and clamor, and evil speaking, be put away from you, with all malice."

Her eyes opened and she groped for the pistol.

"You won't need it," I told her. "Listen to the rest: 'And

be ye kind one to another, tenderhearted, forgiving one another, even as God for Christ's sake hath forgiven you.' Those are the words of Paul and it's all part of God's word, right here—"

"I know what a Bible is," she said, sitting up and scuttling a few feet away from me.

"I thought you would. Farm families always read their Bibles, North or South. I showed it so you would trust me."

"You a Yankee preacher?"

"Yes. Remember the two Yankee soldiers you saw this morning?"

She stiffened, looked at the children, then out the door.

"Yes, they're here. They may look rough but they're good men. They have wives and children of their own and they want to help you."

"There are those other men looking for us, too."

"Those two will never look for anybody again. Never."

There was a vengeful satisfaction in my voice that took even me by surprise, and that a man of God should not have, but more than any words I had said before, it broke down suspicion and resentment between us. Her body relaxed, she fingered the sweater and motioned the children over to pick up the toys.

"Thank you for these but did you bring any food?"

At that, Samuel filled the door, holding up a burlap sack as if it were a flag of truce. She tightened, then eased again at the sight of his face. The tenderness and concern were too obvious for any doubts, and I was deeply thankful I had agreed to help them, a feeling magnified when Silas followed, a perfect duplicate in expression of his brother. Elaine, picture two big-shouldered, war-calloused men handing out biscuits, opening tins of salt beef, unwrapping a box of sweets, passing around canteens of water, all with the gentleness and swift eagerness of a new mother, and you will understand why I talked about a shaft of light amid the darkness.

Such intervals are fleeting in wartime, of course, and when we started back on the trail, the despair of these days confronted us once again. We had all crowded into the cart, horses hitched behind, Silas at the reins, Samuel and I with the children in back. The oldest was Dorothea we had learned, and the younger two were Barbara and Silas and yes, we had some fun with "Big Silas" and "Little Silas."

We left the mud trail from the shack and headed north on the road.

"We live the other way," Dorothea said, reaching out to tap Silas's broad back.

"Can't go home now," he answered, brushing his hand over his face as if swatting away a bothersome insect. "We've been there."

She turned to Samuel, then me. "My mother—?"

Earlier, I had guessed that the brothers were dreading this instant so I didn't wait for Samuel's pleading look before taking Dorothea's hands in mine and saying, "Those men did not leave her alive." Her hands tightened sharply, the only reaction.

"Samuel and Silas buried her in the family gravesite, on the little hill behind your house. You'd be all alone in the house now, too dangerous."

"Was it a proper burial, I mean with the right things said?"

"I said what I knew," Silas told her. "I mean, what I say over my men killed in fighting, all I could do."

"You're a real preacher, aren't you?" she asked me, "not just somebody who stuck this little bit of brass on his coat? You're not a whole lot older than I am now that I see you in the daylight."

"I'm twenty-one, Dorothea, a graduate of the Cavalry

Seminary in Providence, Rhode Island, four years there, and I was ordained as a minister in the Rockville, Rhode Island First Baptist Church."

"And the best preacher I've known in three years of war," interjected Silas.

"Will you come to my mother then?"

Both brothers looked up at the sun, measuring the daylight left.

"Bit of a risk, coming back after dark" said Samuel.

"We'll none of us sleep if we don't," replied Silas, turning the horses.

For the second time in less than a week, I stood by a gravesite at twilight intoning verses from Job, Isaiah, Romans and First Thessalonians, passages grown too familiar by now. Scores of boys and a few old men six nights ago, a young mother now. She was thirty-four, Dorothea had told me, comely, kind, hard-working, a cook who could turn a gamy old chicken and some cornbread into a savory meal, a seamstress who could create a Sunday dress out of scraps and bolt-ends, a gardener who could make the hard-scrabble soil yield everything from sweet peas to peonies—in short, a fictional ideal of love and versatility that I knew was real in Dorothea's eyes and probably not very far from the truth in any event. This was a farm wife we were consecrating.

Psalm Twenty-three had been her favorite, as with so many people, and so I closed by reciting, "The Lord is my shepherd, I shall not want; he maketh me to lie down in green pastures, he leadeth me beside the still waters..."

As I spoke, a perverse impulse rose to tear into the mound of fresh dirt with my bare hands, to reach out to this brutalized woman and apologize on behalf of general William Tecumseh Sherman and the entire Union army.

It passed but left outward traces. My voice was loud

and shaky and I knew tears were on my face as I reached the final verse, "Surely goodness and mercy shall follow me all the days of my life, and I will dwell in the house of the Lord forever."

Tears marked the face of Samuel as he cradled Barbara to his chest, and of Silas holding little Silas on his shoulders. Only Dorothea's eyes were dry and I felt her watching me closely.

"You are a decent and honorable man," she told me. Then she said the same to Samuel and Silas. None of us could do any more than look at her helplessly. We walked back to the cart, shadows long, sky darkening, earth still.

I will pray now and write more in the morning.

With deepest love and devotion,
Ellis

December 15, 1864

My Dearest Elaine,

As I was about to begin this letter, Palmer poked his head in the tent flap and said without preamble, "Where in the world did you go with the Ward brothers yesterday?"

"To offer help where it was needed."

"Good. I know it was to Union soldiers or Union supporters this time."

"Why would you presume that?"

"The Wards are two of the most merciless fighters in this army. Any help they give will be to our side."

"What would you say if I told you we helped some Southerners yesterday and not Union supporters, either."

"I would say you were lying except for who you are. How did you get the Wards involved?"

"The Wards got me involved."

"You must have instigated it somehow."

I silently thanked the Lord that he hadn't come in last night when I was tired and emotionally on the edge. A night's sleep made me deliberately patient and I replied, "I understand how you might think that but the fact is, the Wards approached me with everything planned and ready and I simply followed along."

I then gave him a full account of the day's events, purposely holding his gaze when I finished, challenging him.

He regarded me just as levelly, responding, "Children, yes, they cross the boundaries, I grasp that, of course, but Brantley, can you grasp the idea that you did instigate it? Your presence, your reputation, led the Wards to come up with their plan."

"You don't think they would have made another plan if necessary?"

He sighed in frustration. "I've known those men for three years and you've been here what? Two weeks? I know them, Brantley, and you don't."

I thought of Samuel Ward's words, "Five hundred miles of taking, gotta give something back" and I told Palmer, "Evidently, I know a side to them that you've missed and it makes me question if you really know them." Then I added, giving way to an impulse that I should have resisted, "I even question if you really know yourself, Captain."

He stared in surprise, then straightened to a position of attention and spoke in clipped phrases. "That borders on insolence, Chaplain, even insubordination."

"It was provocative, Captain, and I apologize. There was no hostility in the remark, only an attempt to understand."

"You'll do well to control those attempts. Our relationship is now more formal than it was, the real reason I came to see you. On orders of General Sherman, one of my duties will be to keep track of your whereabouts and ensure that you're available to this command when needed."

I stilled the flash of resentment, took a breath and asked, "How will we make that work?"

"In a typical military way. You will report to me each morning, tell me your plans for the day, and report back in the evening to review the day. Verbally will suffice. We can start now."

"I intend to conduct morning prayer meeting in about twenty minutes, then work on my Sunday message, then ride to the rear to see what the Wards have arranged for the children." I looked for some reaction to that but he simply waited, so I concluded, "I'll probably visit with soldiers I meet along the way to do some Bible reading and pray, a normal chaplain activity."

"Good enough, just remember: no more unscheduled adventures, Brantley."

I didn't need to think about my answer. "Everything is scheduled, Captain," I said purposefully, "Everything."

He dismissed the remark with a snap of his fingers, asking, "Do you know how sanctimonious that sounds?" Then he grew thoughtful and added, "But when you say it, it's not sanctimony, is it? It's an inner light that you steer by, come what may."

"Would you prefer a preacher who's a hypocrite?"

"In truth, yes I would. He wouldn't be a peril to this army and to himself." He sighed once more and finished, "Well, just remember that despite what the Lord may schedule, we have an earthly schedule, you and I."

When the tent flap closed behind him, I whispered, "Father, I lean on your will in all things," and went outside for some fresh air. Lambert stood a few feet away, overly busy scouring my eating utensils.

"You'll remind me to report to Captain Palmer each morning and evening? I'm sure you heard our conversation."

"Ear up against the tent wall, to tell you the truth," he sad with a grin, adding, "t'weren't no surprise. Heard about it yesterday from Uncle Billy's orderly. Meaning no disrespect to the captain, but if he sorta made it seem it was Uncle Billy's idea, well, it was the opposite. It was the captain who told Uncle Billy he thought he should keep his eye on you."

Resentment swelled again. What right did Palmer have to insert himself into my affairs? The reaction showed, bringing a tilt of the head and a conspiratorial twist to Lambert's lips as he said, "Always reasons why you couldn't report on a particular day—a sudden funeral in the wagon train, a wedding among the nigras following us, a soldier or even a camp follower feelin' a need to repent, or maybe a touch of dysentery for you. Ain't no limit to the explanations I could give the captain or even better, get one of the general's orderlies to do it—"

"Enough," I interrupted, laughing silently, grateful for the innocently sly young veteran; he had washed away my resentment. "What's my occupation?"

"Ordained preacher, right now a chaplain in the army—I see what you mean. You wear a cross and you got to tell the truth. I respect that, sir." He shook his head, a gesture of sympathy for my being shackled by the demands of truth.

So, my dear, I'm to have a self-anointed watchdog, a curious turn of events which I will now resolve to accept without further irritation. We know Who is in charge and that I will be used for His work, with or without Palmer. More tomorrow,

Your devoted,
Ellis

CHAPTER SIX:

THE STREAM

December 21, 1864

My Sweet Elaine,

I know you'll be as pleased as I am that Dorothea, Barbara and little Silas have been securely berthed by the Ward brothers in a wagon added to a medical supply unit. They're officially invisible but openly doted on by men grateful for these reminders of their own families. They swing the little ones in the air to great shouts of laughter, let them ride the mules or gentler horses and bring them hand-carved toys beyond count. Dorothea opened the wagon-flap to show me a floor covered with wooden dolls and soldier figurines, clever little Jacob's Ladder contraptions, two see-saws and enough play swords to equip a Roman legion.

She herself is treated with gallantry, riding a wooden seat with a cushion and arm rests, the wood still smelling of freshly cut and sanded pine. It's placed at the front flap where she is largely concealed, although she commands a wide view of the outside world in the manner of a princess traveling among commoners. A bright-looking mulatto girl has been recruited from the Negro ranks to provide female companionship and help with laundry and with care for her brother and sister. Soldiers, especially younger ones, come by in a constant flow to offer food or toys or blankets and to assure her they're ready to assist in any way.

In case you see danger in their riding with the army, rest easily: there will be no combat. Fort McAllister, the final defense of Savannah, has fallen and the remaining Confederate forces will escape the city rather than face this lethal Union army. Only the wetlands remain to slow us and then we'll enter peacefully, where the children can be placed and where someone will know how to get word to their father.

All of this left me contented, obviously, although it was tempered considerably by a story told me by the Ward brothers and a few of the other men I stopped to talk with. It's another savage incident, one that occurred a week earlier and a story I would not have recounted, except that I was unexpectedly towed into its aftermath.

I must omit or change names here because the matter is not officially recorded and authenticated, but the account goes this way: the commanding general of an army corps was growing increasingly agitated by the Negroes who attached themselves to his unit, following the troops and even collecting ahead of them at times. They hindered communications and slowed maneuvers against the persistent Confederate skirmishers, so the general had valid reasons for his agitation but no excuse for his solution.

I wrote in a previous letter about the swift-moving tidal streams the army encountered last week.

Approaching an especially treacherous one, he quick-timed his troops through the Negroes at the head of his line, leaving them merged with the rear contingent, five or six hundred men, women and children in all.

The troops then crossed on a pontoon bridge and, when the last of them was ashore, an order was given to cut the bridge loose, stranding the Negroes on the opposite bank. There, they stood defenseless against Confederate troops who would eagerly shoot some and hang some for examples, send others back to their vengeful masters, and scatter the rest to starve in the swamp-ridden countryside.

They saw only one choice: try to get across the racing waters. Some did, clinging to timbers left over from the pontoons, or riding primitive rafts made of logs, or holding tight to those who were strong enough swimmers—some, only some. God alone knows how many others were carried away.

Sad to say, only the handful of men who talked to me about the incident were disturbed by it.

When I mentioned it to others, curious as to the reaction I'd elicit, indifferent shrugs were the answer or hasty glances around, with advice to keep it to myself.

To his everlasting credit, an officer in the corps—I'll call him Major Jeremy Conover—would not let the matter rest. He knew there was no point in trying to enlist Sherman's help. You don't bring unwelcome distractions to a general preoccupied with moving sixty thousand men and their equipment through the serpentine marshes, rice fields and canals that guard Savannah. Moreover, Sherman was dashing between the camps of three armies right now: his own two and that of General John Foster, who had just landed a division by sea on the South Carolina coast.

Conover's plan was to ride back through the ranks, find every witness he could and collect their statements into a detailed letter of protest to the Senate Military Committee. He also planned to send the letter to a friend with influence at the leading newspapers.

I learned all this from Conover himself when he appeared before my tent at dawn today, accompanied by three other sympathetic officers from the corps. "Would I join them?" he asked, noting that "a chaplain's presence would be beneficial in an inquiry like this one."

He was a lean, hook-nosed man draped nearly to his boots in a black poncho—a steady December rain was falling—and he had alert dark eyes that met mine candidly, acknowledging what was in both our minds: having Sherman's chaplain along, and as a signatory to the letter, would imply the general's support. And of course, there was the unspoken persuasion. He had heard that I was enough of a maverick to take action if I believed the cause was just. These, at least, were my impressions at the time and they were correct as far as they went. I was to learn by day's end that Conover had a deeper purpose.

He had correctly judged my willingness to act, of course, but he didn't know my Palmer arrangement. I needed to bypass the captain, which took a moment's thought—only a moment, I confess—and then I embarked on one of those little deceits that men of God should avoid, and that certainly should not have given me the satisfaction I felt when I quietly entered the block of headquarters tents, confirmed that Sherman was away and sought out General Slocum, the next-ranking officer.

Slocum had continued to ignore me since our introduction—nothing personal, I knew; battle plans and logistics consumed all his attention—and he never even looked up from a table full of dispatches when I told him Major Conover needed me today. He gestured approval as if shooing a fly. I raced back to my tent to tell Lambert to find Captain Palmer and inform the captain where I would be, at General Slocum's orders. Neither of us broke a smile, but we both knew that Lambert would have a rollicking good time telling his colleagues how I played the "general's orders" game back at Palmer.

The mission itself disappointed me. A whole day's riding and interviewing unearthed only five soldiers willing to describe the tragic stream crossing and then put their names to their statements. At one point, having stopped to remove some twigs from my horse's fetlocks, I was about a hundred feet from one of Conover's interviews. The scene before me was typical: a lone trooper hunched over against the rain, surrounded by officers batlike in their ponchos, while knots of other soldiers observed, most with faces set in grim and suspicious lines, knowing questions were being asked that could tarnish the reputation of an entire corps.

Even those who had talked with me two days earlier never came forward for the major. It's one thing to speak to a young chaplain passing through, quite another to attach your name to a document that would travel all the way to a senate committee and quite possibly appear in newspapers. That we had as many as five was evidence of the cruelty at the stream.

Among the Negroes, it was different, although still less than we might have hoped. Even in their tattered, ill-treated ranks there was fear of being identified and singled out for return to their former owners or retaliation from soldiers of the corps. Some twenty-one spoke to us, many with searing memories of loved ones being carried off by the current, including women with children in their arms.

Once again, I will spare you details, except to say there were so many accounts of loss and bravery we could have compiled a volume—and all of it with little hope of making an impact. These were colored people, illiterate and unreliable in the eyes of cosmopolitan Washington. A few senators might be moved by their suffering but the majority would probably not even take the time to read this part of Conover's report.

You may imagine that my spirits were low as we returned and yet, to my surprise, the others rode straight in their saddles, looking confident and calm, the major even whistling little melodies from time to time. I presumed this is how professional soldiers handle a disappointing foray and raised myself from the discouraged slump that had overtaken me.

The rain ended and a gauzy moon was high when we finally dismounted at headquarters. Conover shook my hand and said cheerfully, "Your presence was of immeasurable help, Chaplain. I mean to write a letter of commendation to General Sherman. God bless you for joining us today."

In front of my tent, no surprise, Palmer waited, seated on my camp chair, puffing crisp little cloudlets into the air from a small meerschaum. He considered their upward flight serenely for a few moments before pointing the stem of the pipe at me, asking, "Why that little subterfuge with Slocum this morning?"

I told him simply, "I assumed you'd refuse permission."

He looked into the embers of his pipe and said, almost to himself, "I wonder if we'll ever understand each other." Shaking his head, he went on, "This was an organized mission under the command of a veteran officer. I have no problem with that. It's when you go dashing off on your own, like you did after the Negro with the drum, or with the Ward brothers, or when you took that rebel boy in Hillardville to the hospital, right in front of troops who certainly didn't need any more provoking—those are the little crusades that could cause real trouble for people around you, for military goals, for yourself." He shook the meerschaum at me for emphasis, then added, "Well, at least you accomplished something today."

"Not really, I'm afraid, although Major Conover put a brave face on it."

"How could it fail?" he asked, looking genuinely startled.

I explained how few people were willing to testify and he just stared at me, then stood up and laughed aloud.

"Brantley," he said, "there are times when you are so naïve, you're a real treasure."

Pointing the pipe again, he continued, "I want you to review the actions of your little group today and see if you can find some good in it. As Uncle Billy would say, think it through."

I recalled Sherman saying those words that night on the bluff and I felt as juvenile as I did then, but I conjured up the events of the day like a series of pictures: the announcements Conover made, the few who responded, the eyes of the troops on us as we rode by, the rapid way they made room on the trails, the way they stared at the interviews we conducted, the stiff and nervous reactions of the officers we encountered—the eyes of the troops on us—the stiff and nervous reactions of the officers—

"You understand it now, don't you?" Palmer asked.

"I understand nobody in that corps, from the commanding general on down, will ever do anything again like they did at the stream."

"Exactly. That's the point of Conover's strategy, not the report, which he'll send, of course, but in military terms the report was only a feint. The real purpose was to blaze a trail through the corps, to make certain every man was aware that somebody was watching and there would be severe consequences in the future. But Conover's one of the smartest men in this army and he aimed higher than that. He wanted to ride with a sword of truth at his side and that, my innocent young seminarian, was you."

"I was a wet kitchen rag in the saddle today, nobody's sword of truth."

"Even in this bit of moonlight, I can see your lapel cross shining. I presume Conover took great care to introduce you at every stop today, am I right?"

I recalled that the major had even presented me ahead of his own officers. I told Palmer so.

"Do you know why?" he asked.

"Because people think I have some direct line to General Sherman, which I don't, as you know."

"Outside of headquarters, people don't know that. But that's only a small part of it. What Conover really needed was your unique reputation: the chaplain who preaches from the heart every Sunday, the chaplain who actually leads prayer meetings, the chaplain who never steals, the chaplain who never drinks, the chaplain who never gambles, the chaplain who will walk into a shack to rescue some children even though he knows there's a girl with a pistol inside—you don't suppose the Ward brothers didn't talk about that—the troops even tolerate your willingness to help a Negro or a Rebel boy, although I wouldn't recommend you repeat any of those actions. The point is, they see in you a true man of God, a man who will do his best to emulate Christ here on earth."

He came close again, pipestem against my chest, and said, "Without you, the major had a military inquiry that let people know they had violated army directives and he was watching them. With you, he had a divine inquiry to let people know they had violated heavenly directives and God was watching them."

He poked me twice and added, "In short, without you, Connolly could make people afraid. With you, he could also make them ashamed. Do you know the power of those two emotions working together? Do you see your role now?"

I took a few seconds to digest it, then said, "Yes, I rode among men trained to kill as an emblem of Christ's commandment to love one another."

It was his turn to take a few seconds, then he said "Love one another, yes." He rose to leave and added, with his back to me, "Keep reminding us, Parson."

Later, I tried to remember if those parting words had his customary sardonic edge and I couldn't decide, so maybe they were sincere. I'll pray they were.

It's likely we'll be moving on Savannah tomorrow. Wagons were tightly packed and units were shuffling into formation as we returned. These moves are always pre-dawn affairs, so I'll get some sleep now, content that I'm a little less naïve than when this day began and, I suppose, somewhat less of a treasure.

Always your loving and devoted,
Ellis

CHAPTER SEVEN:

SAVANNAH

December 27, 1864

My Sweet Elaine,

Some saddening news; perhaps you read it in the newspapers: General Sherman has lost another son. You know about the eight-year-old who visited headquarters last year and contracted an illness that proved fatal. Another tragedy has now struck: a six-month old whom he had never seen fell to an infancy disease at home. When the word came, he called for me to sit and pray and he was as quiet as I have ever seen him, no tears, of course, and then he made the melancholy remark that when he was a boy, his father died and now that he's a father, his boys are dying. Death surrounding me, he said, spreading his hands to indicate the battlefield, too.

I talked about God's will and about Job and he listened, then admitted he was not a man of any great spiritual side. He revealed some private history: he was born and raised a Presbyterian but his father's death left eleven children behind, more than his mother could handle, so he was taken in by friends, a Catholic family, obliging him to absorb new doctrines, new worship habits. The outcome was a large measure of indifference to religious practices. He came to Sunday services as an example for the troops although, he told me, my sermons were drawing them now as much as his presence and even he found it more natural, less of an obligation, to be there.

He seemed impatient and annoyed with himself towards the end. Calling a chaplain and talking of personal matters was unusual, I'm sure, and not something a man like Sherman would be comfortable with. On balance though, I think he was satisfied with the time together. I know I was, welcoming any chance to plant God's word.

I'm no longer awed in Sherman's presence, another benefit of this meeting. We're all one before God, I know, but how can the gulf between a young chaplain and a commanding general not be intimidating? It's bridged now because my heart is reached; sorrow truly makes us all one.

To move on to better news: the march into Savannah was as peaceful as anticipated. The place is quiet and beautiful for the most part and a home has been found for the children with an Episcopal priest, the reverend Malcolm Witherspoon, a man who is generous one moment, quarrelsome the next and I will try to explain the contradiction later.

The city is a welcome respite, an Eden compared to our other stops, and yet, my sweet Elaine, I can't dissolve the ache of wanting you beside me. If there is one time that I miss you more than another, this is that time. A Christmas season without you is an emotional amputation—and once again, I will stop myself. You know the depth of our commitment to one another and if I descend into a dejected longing—a form of self-pity, really—it does neither of us any good. I will trust our Lord to reunite us in His time.

And now I must tell you I am writing with a measure of embarrassment, knowing you are toiling through a Rhode Island winter, knowing that you step outside bundled in sweaters, overcoat, scarves and mittens, your boots laced tightly against the snow, an icy wind at your face, and I? I am sitting barefoot on a veranda of Reverend Witherspoon's vicarage, unbuttoned cotton field jacket my heaviest garment, while a light sea breeze brushes my cheek.

You will be teasing me for years about this, won't

you? But there's nothing I can do about the climate here, chilly enough for a blanket at night and warm enough for swimming the next day. Many of the troops are actually diving and splashing about in the Savannah river as I write. Others are strolling the avenues, wide and well-paved thoroughfares shaded by evergreen oaks, with miniature parks at almost every intersection. Soldiers and citizens mingle courteously enough. It's one of the benefits of the space all around. While the streets are crowded, their width, the inviting parks, and the open water close by all give a sense of room, unlike the oppressive crowding that incited the riots at Hillardville.

I was warned by Reverend Witherspoon that some treacherous weather lay ahead. Heavy rain, high winds and sharp drops in temperature are common this time of year. For now, however, the climate is balmy, and the good spirits are lifted even higher by the arrival of food from the ships, abundant enough to be shared with the populace, supplemented by Savannah warehouses full of rice that Confederate forces were holding for themselves and that Sherman has now distributed. The river here also produces oysters in endless supply. "You can just go scoop them out!" I heard from a happy Indiana trooper whose Christmas dinner included oyster soup, oysters on the half-shell, oyster stew, oysters fried and oysters roasted.

The navy also brought new clothes, with shoes and boots particularly welcome, and so I found myself celebrating Christmas Eve with contented, well-fed, well-garbed officers and men. We assembled at a place called Forsyth Park, a suitable expanse of lawn except for a flowing fountain at its entrance, a pedestal-like affair supporting a sculpture of a robust female figure in the Greek style (meaning rather carelessly draped) and surrounded by statuettes of tritons, sea gods who were half-man, half-serpent, and, like the female, half-clad.

It brought a sour squint from General Howard as he entered, ever-present Bible under his arm, then a shrug and some words called out to me, "Think of Corinth, Preacher." And so for an instant, with salty air in my nostrils, this modern seaport of Savannah became the ancient seaport of Corinth and Chaplain Brantley became the Apostle Paul, planting the banner of Christ in the very center of Grecian decadence, a mental indulgence I brushed away easily but I tell you all this—the climate, the park, the statuary, my silly imagining—with a point: the simple truth, which I was about to relate, overcomes all surroundings.

I faced a somewhat restless congregation at the start, something I had prepared for, recognizing that even Christmas Eve could not totally dampen the liveliness of soldiers suddenly released from combat into safety and comfort. My thought was to get them singing, so Lambert had rounded up some guitarists and vocalists to lead and, after welcoming everybody, I called for "Hark, the Herald Angels" and then, "O Come, O Come, Emmanuel," whose third verse, as you know, cites "the rod of Jesse."

When I asked, "Who can recite a Bible verse that inspired these words?" hands showed everywhere. The question, of course, served to focus attention (who would I choose?) and you'll forgive me, I know, for such an old classroom tactic. I pointed to a young private who was bouncing up and down with eagerness. He stood and shouted, "Isaiah, Chapter Eleven, the first verse, 'And there shall come forth a rod out of the stem of Jesse, and a branch shall grow out of his roots!'"

I repeated the words instantly, loudly and quickly, to forestall applause from his comrades and then said them once more with deliberation and reverence. The restlessness—shuffling and joking among the troops—was barely discernible now, so I could speak undistracted about the lineage of Jesus, and of the many Old Testament prophesies of the Messiah's coming, making the transition to the gospel of Luke a natural one—and do those verses of Luke's ever lose their power?

The story of Zacharias and Elizabeth, the birth and naming of John, the story of Mary and Joseph, the angelic visits, Mary's glorious prayer, the trek to Bethlehem—to these roughened travelers before me, I explained how arduous the ninety miles to Bethlehem would have been, all stony roads, valleys, deserts and steep hills, and they sat up, understanding it—and then, in a manger, the birth of Christ, the starry night, the shepherds, the celestial choir—I ask again, these verses, do they ever lose their power? From the mid-point—when I reached Mary's words, "For He hath regarded the low estate of his handmaiden: for behold, from henceforth all generations shall call me blessed,"—from then on, the stillness was total, every eye and every ear was attuned to the message, held fast by the eternal truth of this night.

Torches were lit by now and we closed with the sweet new hymn, "Silent Night, Holy Night," filling the dusk with the melody, singing through it twice at the demand of the troops and, following a final prayer, we dispersed, walking hushed through the streets, now misty with a light seaborne rain. Nobody congratulated me and I was grateful. This was our Savior's night, not mine.

The Ward brothers found a haven for Dorothea, Barbara and little Silas by the simple expedient of walking through town, looking for a church that was "sizable, but didn't fuss too much about grass and flower beds and such."

I unraveled the reasoning and admired it. "Sizable" meant enough resources to offer shelter. "Didn't fuss too much" meant none of the vanity that turns so many church grounds into showplaces. Lack of vanity was a sign of good character, and if you see one sign you should see others, like compassion for three displaced children.

This homespun logic led them to Saint Thomas Episcopal Church, a three-story building of scoured red brick and vaulted, delicately figured stained glass windows, a place that bespoke means, with neatly trimmed grass and a line of low shrubbery nestled up to the building as an adjunct to the church, not a competition for attention.

"See that?" asked Samuel as we—the brothers, the children and I—reached the front steps. "Nothing fancy and Reverend Witherspoon, well, he can be a little irritable but he talks plain, like you."

"Looks like a pigeon, though," Silas chuckled.

"Well, I see some hawk in him when he gets prickly," countered Samuel.

"That, too," admitted Silas. "But that was when we mentioned you were General Sherman's chaplain. Maybe we shouldn't have done that, but you'll manage it, Preacher."

The brothers had spoken earlier with Reverend Witherspoon, gaining no commitment, only agreement to meet the children and "that young chaplain." They hadn't mentioned "irritable" or needing some managing until now and it suddenly occurred to me that they hadn't mentioned where they talked.

"Were you inside the church?" I asked.

"No," Samuel said, "he was just coming in so we talked right here on the steps. Is that important?"

"Have you been in an Episcopal church before?"

"No, we went to the Lutheran church at home, big as this one."

"I'm sure it was simple inside, though. This church might be more elegant on the inside than you expect."

It was even more so than I expected. Dorothea, Barbara and little Silas immediately drew tight to one another when we entered, while the Ward brothers turned here and there like weather vanes trying to absorb it all. Saint Thomas was cathedral-like, a particularly imposing example of Anglican church design, with a timbered ceiling arching high overhead and roseate light from the stained glass playing over polished mahogany pews, carpeted aisles, statues in wall niches, a massive pipe organ, a two-tiered choir gallery contained within intricately carved railings and, under a flying buttress, an elevated chancel that seemed a mile away (yes, Elaine, I fought back a fleeting desire to preach from that vantage point). Add the hushed sound that accompanies such a Gothic setting and you can see how intimidated the children would be after the pinewood churches of the countryside. To depend on the pastor of this place was an uncertain prospect at best, especially knowing that the army, with their protectors, would soon be gone.

Reverend Witherspoon was at the reading desk, a lectern-sized Bible open before him, mouthing words into the air, one hand raised, an obvious sermon preparation. He kept on for two or three minutes, breathed an audible "Amen," and descended with measured steps to meet us in the wide center aisle.

"Chaplain Brantley," he repeated when Samuel introduced us, bowing with a quick head motion, then stepping back as if to keep some distance between us and asking, "Fresh out of seminary?"

He was no taller than my shoulder, he was a bit plump,

his gray hair lay flat to his ears, his eyes were prominent and wideset and, wearing a white surplice, he did resemble a pigeon. In his stance, however, was the hawk that Samuel spotted: head and shoulders thrust forward, body taut, ready to pounce on a false word or any hint of Northern trickery.

"Three months," I answered, "but the last month has been with the army, which adds a lot of age in a short time." It was a bit brash considering he was my senior by perhaps forty years and he blinked at it, then said, "Baptist seminary, correct?"

"Calvary Baptist, Providence, Rhode Island. Does a lack of humility give it away?" I tried a smile which he didn't return.

"From seminarian to Sherman's chaplain is quite a leap. It would take some ambition and aggressiveness. Unless you're related to the general?"

"No relation, and it was pure accident. His chaplain took sick—"

"He heard Pastor Brantley preach, the general did," cut in Samuel, "all the convincing he needed."

"Please," said the reverend and it was a sound of disdain. "A Union army sermon. I can just hear it. Hollering and shouting all the way, thumping the lectern, waving the Bible, we're Joshua, we're David, we're an army of God, let's get the infidels! You work the troops into blood-thirsty savagery in the name of the Lord."

"No!" interrupted Samuel, and the word echoed in the open chamber.

"All wrong," said Silas, putting a cautionary hand on his brother. Then, with an unexpected touch of poetry, he went on, "Sure, he'll be the voice of thunder on the mountaintop sometimes, you can't whisper if you're quoting Isaiah, say, and he can also speak as gentle as Mary quieting the Babe, and he can give you all the voices in between but it's always real, no acting, always from his heart, and never a blood-thirsty word. He's a true Christian, Reverend. He shows it by what he says and he shows it by what he does."

Where his brother had displayed anger, Silas was simply impassioned, almost pleading for the reverend's understanding. The brothers had not been present for my warlike speech before the one-sided battle at Danner's Crossing. I recalled it with some guilt, along with gratitude for Silas's words.

Reverend Witherspoon drew his head back and blinked again, thrust his head forward once more and said to me "You've evidently got an orator's gift, and I'll take the sergeant's word for your virtues. Why then should you serve Sherman so closely? You may not be blood-thirsty but he certainly is."

"Yes, he is, at times. So may we all be, God save us. And yet, I have looked at a peaceful town in the moonlight with him and heard him lament that he would have to attack it the next day, so there is another side."

"We're all complicated, young man. However, not all of us make war a career. At heart, what sort of man does that, and does it successfully?"

Again, I tried to communicate what I only sensed and didn't really know. "A man with more war in his heart than most of us, I can't deny that, a man who can contemplate the letting of blood by friends and enemies alike, and in large numbers, and still give the orders to march into battle. And also a man who has lost two sons and who grieves privately with a chaplain for ten minutes and goes right back to war—but the grief remains, for the children, for the dead soldiers, North and South, probably even grief for who he is and what he must do."

"Two sons? I've heard of only one."

It was odd to fasten on that point among all I had said

and I wondered what losses he might have suffered. I told him about Sherman's infant and he made a little grunting sound, nothing else, then asked, "You've seen death in the field by now?"

"Yes."

"Performed burial services?"

"For soldiers, Union and Confederate, and for the mother of these children."

He had looked at the children briefly when the Wards introduced us and had paid no attention since. "Tell me their story," he said, still without looking their way.

"We were moving through the swamp country west of here," Samuel began and Reverend Witherspoon held a hand up, impatiently. "Not you, Sergeant. I want it from the chaplain." He shifted around as if regretting his tone but offered no apology.

I told him all of it as plainly as I could, keeping my voice flat, trying to avoid any hint of emotion before this critical man for fear he would perceive it as false. I thought I succeeded until, at my recounting the burial service on the little hill beyond the farm, I saw him blink again several times, take in a breath and look at me solemnly. I suppose there is no unemotional way to tell about Dorothea and her sister and brother and, finally, he turned to them.

Leaning over to little Silas he asked, as calmly as if they had been chatting all afternoon, "Do you eat catfish?"

"Tew," came the response.

"He's saying stew," explained Dorothea.

"I figured." To Barbara, he said, "And how do you feel about catfish stew?"

She bobbed her head up and down.

"Do you like it with sassafras leaves?"

She bobbed again, looking up for agreement from Dorothea, who murmured "Yes," watching the reverend rather than her sister and all at once her shoulders, which had been stiff and hunched up, visibly loosened.

To Dorothea, he said, "Many folks don't know this but you can put chunks of sausage in catfish stew. I think it's Yankees mainly who don't know that. You probably know all about it."

"Used to do it when we could get the sausage. You could put chicken in, too, really good if you fry it first to crisp it up."

"You should have a little cooking talk with my housekeeper. You'd both have a good time. She's right across the lane in the vicarage, the house I live in, so suppose we all walk over, see what's on the stove for dinner, show you around the house. It's big, with verandas and balconies, even some rooms you might like to stay in for a time."

And so we found ourselves following Reverend Witherspoon, still chatting with the children, somehow finding a second to throw a dismissive glance at me that said "Could you have done this so smoothly, young man?" It was a needless little poke and I debated whether the fault were mine. Am I overly bold for my years? Is my association with Sherman too irritating for him?

In any event, the vital question of finding shelter for the children was answered, and quite well. The vicarage is a comfortable brick manse of at least a dozen rooms, all sun-filled and spacious and all opening on one of the verandas or balconies the reverend mentioned. The housekeeper, Mrs. Finch, proved motherly and talkative once she grasped that these Yankees were actually helping three Georgia children. Two servant girls employed in the household are only a little older than Dorothea and they befriended her instantly, while the two little ones, of course, were the targets of more fussing and tickling and hugging than was probably good for them.

After a simple but filling meal of chicken and shrimp, and a catfish gumbo Mrs. Finch seemed to whip out of nowhere when little Silas asked for "Tew," Reverend Witherspoon surprised me by inviting me to stay and talk and even spend the night. "If General Sherman can spare you," he added.

Living quarters are informal right now. Sherman is staying at a wealthy cotton merchant's mansion and other officers are billeted at various homes around the city, so there was nothing to hold me back except the reverend's attitude and I felt that, despite the Sherman barb, he was sincere, or at least his code of Southern hospitality made the invitation genuine. The Wards would be able to tell Lambert where I was and Lambert could inform Captain Palmer if he chose.

We talked, Reverend Witherspoon and I, until well past midnight, starting with Bible readings from Daniel and Micah, and then moving on to John, Acts and Romans, reading with the exhilaration the Word always brings, finally closing our Bibles, holding them as firmly as knights of old held their lances, ready now for the verbal combat to come...and come it did, with the first thrust from my host in the form of an invitation, actually a challenge, to attend communion at Saint Thomas, and so we were quickly engaged in a sharp theological jousting over communion and then over baptism. Were they ordinances? Were they sacraments? Did they bestow grace? If so, wasn't that salvation by works, contrary to Paul's teachings? Is transubstantiation a credible interpretation of the words of Jesus at The Last Supper? Does the wafer and the wine really become His body and blood? Don't the words of Jesus, "The flesh profiteth nothing," settle the matter? On we went, sweeping through the doctrinal disputes, disputes I have debated in the past with buoyancy and enthusiasm.

Tonight, however, was different. Reverend Witherspoon charged in energetically enough at first but mid-way became spiritless, making his arguments seemingly by rote while his mind roamed elsewhere, revealed in occasional little pauses as he evidently tried to recapture a train of thought, and revealed in absent-minded tapping of his feet and, disturbingly, in some hawk-like glances at me that I took to be involuntary; he'd catch himself and look away quickly.

My usual enthusiasm faded in reaction. When one of the servant girls peered in to ask if we would care for some tea and plum cake, I was ready to call a halt.

The reverend clearly felt the same and so we agreed on God's sovereignty in all matters divine and doctrinal, and settled back, watching the tea and cake being wheeled in on a gleaming Colonial dining cart and then served on a dainty china set, pale blue and embossed with roses.

I usually pay no attention to such things, as you well know, but in this case it was one of the few womanly touches in what was otherwise an austerely furnished home of pine or cherrywood items, well-made but unadorned, calling to mind one of the prosperous but thrifty farmhouses at home. The decorative touches—lace curtains, a colorful vase, small braided rugs, an embroidered cushion here and there—were all placed with care, never obtrusive, always contributing to the simplicity of the whole.

My eyes must have been roving about the room, for Reverend Witherspoon remarked, "This place used to be overstuffed with brocaded sofas and settees and Persian carpeting and silken drapes. Queen Elizabeth herself could have lived here. The priest before me thought a rich-looking vicarage was in keeping with the church."

"And you thought it contended with the church."

"Certainly. When you shepherd a church won't your vicarage—parsonage—be simple and modest?"

"So will the church."

"Ah, yes, that bare-bones Puritan ideal, nothing to distract from the word of God. I want you to visualize Madonna of the Magnificat—you know, the glorious painting by Boticelli of the angel Gabriel speaking to Mary. If you came into possession of it, would you tack it up on the wall, bare canvas, nothing to set it apart? I doubt that. You'd find a beautiful frame to make it clear this is unique, this deserves your complete attention. I believe we have to treat the word of God that way, especially for the doubters and the new believers and the children, those who will relate the majesty of God to the majesty of their surroundings."

A torrent of objections ran through my mind: no painting, whatever its beauty, lives and grows in the heart as the Word does; trying to frame God's word is like trying to contain the Mississippi at flood crest; making the church so majestic leaves the impression God's word dwells only here and you're free to ignore it elsewhere, none of which I said aloud. We had argued enough already and his manner intrigued me more than his words. He was fervent and intense, bending half out of his chair toward me when he spoke of "the majesty of their surroundings."

"You love that church, don't you?" I asked. I had been weighing my words previously but this was spontaneous.

"I presume you're not accusing me of worshiping a building instead of our Lord." The hawk had surfaced in an angry stretch of the head toward me and an unblinking stare.

"Not for a second. The church is a means to reach your flock and you preach the gospel to them with a full heart. If you were convinced that giving up the church would save one soul, you would do it. But it would be a wrenching sacrifice, wouldn't it, like losing a loved one?"

The anger left, the head receded and he asked me, "How old are you, nineteen, twenty?"

"Twenty-one."

"Twenty-one. God has gifted you with unusual perception." He rose and began circling the room slowly, speaking to the walls and floor as much as to me.

"Five years before you were born, I came to Saint Thomas, a new parish priest with a young wife and a newborn son, Malcolm junior. My wife adored the rich furniture that was left by the old priest. Nevertheless, when I said we must simplify, she helped me without a word of protest and the house you see here today is her doing—the plain rocking chair you sit in, the fine teacup you hold, the balance throughout—her doing. That's only one example of the helpmeet she was. You understand how a priest's wife, a pastor's wife, gives her life to the needs of the congregation: the women's ministries, the meetings, the counseling, the visits to the sick, the Sunday School, the teas, the dinners, along with a mother's work in raising a son."

"Endless," I replied, thinking of you, with thanks to God.

"Malcolm grew tall and straight as you are," he continued, "a boy and then a man who returned all the love he received. We enjoyed each other's company at all times, which sounds insignificant but do you know what a sign of love it is? How rare and precious it is among parents and children?"

"I think I do."

He stood still now, waiting for the question that had to be asked, making it my responsibility. "Where are they now?"

He resumed circling, looking directly at me this time and answered, "My son died two months ago in Maryland, in the Lookout Point prisoner of war camp. You know of it?"

"Yes."

"You know the conditions there?"

"I've heard about them." He waited for more, as if this were a confessional. "The conditions are inhuman, no sanitation, rotting scraps of food, no medicines, guards who beat prisoners unmercifully—Negro guards, assigned in spite to oversee white Southerners."

"In malice," he corrected me.

Once again, I held my thoughts. There was no point in mentioning Andersonville or the other Confederate camps where Union soldiers were equally maltreated; cruelty does not excuse cruelty.

"He was wounded and captured at Chattanooga by your General Sherman's troops, who stole his watch, a present from his mother and me, and his money, his shoes and even his belt buckle and then they sent him off untreated in a railroad grain car to Maryland. That was November, a year ago, so he endured eleven months, that's three hundred thirty-six days—I counted like a man obsessed—three hundred thirty-six days of that prison. Yes, you'll tell me General Sherman knew nothing about it. I'll tell you if that's all the discipline he exercises, he's a barbarian."

I remembered the out-of-control rioters at Hillardville and made no comment. Instead, I asked, "And Mrs. Witherspoon?"

"She held on for three weeks after the news came. She had one of those irregular heartbeats all her life, never bothered her much, but the doctor blamed it for her passing, put it in the report that way. How do you write broken-hearted mother in a medical report?"

Again, I had no comment, only another question.

"And that leaves the church?"

"Twenty-six years with three loves: my wife, my boy, the church. That does not deny my God. He is my abiding passion and He will carry me through this. What you must understand is how fresh, how new these injuries are. Two of the three cornerstones of my earthly life are gone, so yes, that leaves the church, and gives you the answer to the question, 'You love that church, don't you?' God has brought war to this land, brought it home to me, and I'm human enough to treasure and cling to the one possession He has left me."

I stood up myself now and walked to a glass-paned door that led to a veranda, looking out, not seeing anything, my back to him. "And human enough," I said, "to resent someone in this blue uniform suddenly appearing in the church you love, and more than the uniform, someone directly tied to Sherman, the personification of all that has fallen on you."

Turning to face him, I said, "My staying under your roof is an offense to you. The code of hospitality doesn't require you to go that far. I thank you, Reverend, for your generosity toward the children and your courtesy to the Wards and myself. I'll say goodnight, sir, and return to my post."

To my complete surprise, that brought a smile, the first I'd seen, and he shook his finger at me as one might do to an erring child. "And I thought you were perceptive, young man. Don't you see that inviting you here is a healing step for me? Yes, a Yankee chaplain under my roof, and Sherman's own chaplain, at that. Yes, it grinds at me, which is why I knew I must do it the moment you walked into this house. Do you see God's hand in it? Do you see the perfect opportunity He's granted me to begin redemption and restoration?" He shook the finger again to underscore the point and turned to leave, calling back, "Sleep well, Chaplain. Breakfast is at seven."

As you would expect from what I've told you so far, breakfast was traditional and excellent: fried eggs, hominy (salt and butter turns it tasty), cornbread still hot and the best coffee I've had since leaving home. Dorothea appeared less somber and the little ones squirmed and giggled and put away mounds of food that looked bigger than they did.

No mention was made of last night's conversation. Our morning talk was of recipes, the behavior of children, and the differences in farming the fertile soils of Georgia, the grassy fields of New England and the rocky hills of Scotland. Reverend Witherspoon is from an unpronounceable farming village near Edinburgh and he reminisced about his boyhood adventures caring for chickens and geese, imitating some of their antics for the benefit of Barbara and little Silas, innocently unaware that he resembled a fluttering pigeon no matter which fowl he mimicked. It was immensely satisfying to hear them laugh—Dorothea as loud as the little ones, although I sensed some of it was forced for their benefit—and to see Reverend Witherspoon so light-hearted after the frictions of the day before.

He and I are sitting on opposite ends of the veranda now, each occupied with writing—for him, a letter to Dorothea's father that he will copy several times, praying one of the copies will arrive; for me, this letter to you, which I confess I had to interrupt a minute ago as the stained glass windows of the church across the lane caught my attention. They cover the entire side of the building and the sun had just come over the vicarage roof to strike lambent blues and reds and golds into them, illuminating the heavenly figures etched into the glass, shifting from panel to panel, now and then striking such brilliance the eye had to look away, as if shrinking from the glory of God.

We both understand it's no more than the scientific properties of light and glass on display, and you and I will never build such a church, but it was impressive, and it brought a serene, almost beatific look to Reverend Witherspoon. I'm sure he and Mrs.Witherspoon and Malcolm shared the sight regularly, and if he shared it again with them this morning, can we find fault with that?

Your devoted,
Ellis

CHAPTER EIGHT:
BURIALS

January 5, 1865

My Dearest Elaine,

If my penmanship is unsteady, the swells of the Atlantic Ocean are to blame. I'm writing from the stern of the USS Cambridge, a steam cruiser en route from Savannah to Norfolk, where I am to be stationed. A crewman has lashed a barrel to a stanchion as a seat for me and found a small plank to be a lap desk and now he, and some shipmates, are strolling around casually, waiting for me to be seasick. They know nothing of Rhode Island and what it's like to sail Narragansett Bay with the wind up. The Atlantic holds no terror after that, especially in this solid vessel, more than eight hundred tons I'm told, compared to the skiff we would take out, a rather foolhardy thing to do, excusable in two young people in love—

I know, I'm blathering, once again trying to delay writing of distressing events, events that involve Palmer. Palmer, who cautioned me the morning we watched the burning of the railroad tracks. Do you remember that letter? His warning about how suddenly lives can be changed forever?

I'll explain what has happened, and continue in the narrative style I've been using, so that you may understand events as they unfolded and, I pray, understand with a forgiving heart.

You will recall that in my last letter from Savannah I called the city peaceful and beautiful for the most part. Sadly, I now must tell you of the other part. Circumstances forced me into it and since it has to be described, I will plunge ahead. No preamble will make it any less distasteful.

By the riverfront, houses are to be found that provide women, liquor and gambling to visiting seafarers and to those townsmen of lustful mind. Dark alleyways and railroad embankments with shadowy niches offer more cover for everything illicit; in short, an ugly, ugly quarter of town.

Obviously, such a place and an army in from the field were ripe for each other and the inevitable happened—not that everyone succumbed; indeed, most seem to have resisted but even a fraction of an army so big added up to lines of men before these houses, and I do mean lines, as if entering a fairground, except joy and camaraderie give way to pushing and shoving and swearing and the basest of jokes and songs. The navy brought in payrolls as well as food and clothes, so all temptations were affordable, heavy gambling among them. Knots of men at poker and dice crowded the intersections and the public parts of the railroad embankments, the hopeful steadily fleeced by the shrewd, all of it eased along by the liquor that flowed as freely as the nearby river.

There was no point in my asking why this is countenanced. I'd be told the men need the relief and I was foolish even to raise the matter, but at dinner with Palmer and several other officers, including a Major Nims, who was serving as provost, I did wonder aloud about the effect on military readiness and discipline.

"They'll be restored," replied the major. "Uncle Billy won't let this go on too long."

"How long is too long?"

"Now don't ask military men a moral question," Palmer cut in. "It confuses us." He drew a round of friendly laughter.

"A week, maybe two," the major said. "He'll want the men off the streets by then, getting themselves and their equipment ready to move on South Carolina."

"Won't it be like stopping runaway horses?"

"Only the wilder element. Some forceful measures are always needed there and I'll have platoons ready, but you know the men by now, Chaplain. The great majority are simply good soldiers letting off pressure and they'll respond."

"I think the chaplain is planning to go there and preach," offered a lieutenant.

"A sermon with whiskey bottles flying at you," said another. "Now there's a challenge, Chaplain."

"Better stop your teasing," cautioned Major Nims. "He's just reckless enough to try it and good enough to get away with it."

"I have to disappoint everybody," I told them. "My reckless days are over. Ask Captain Palmer."

Palmer began to whistle "Now Thank We All Our God," evoking more laughter, all of it amiable and I let myself grow relaxed amid the food and genial company, putting aside thoughts of the riverfront debauchery and my inability to confront it.

Three hours later, I was galloping to confront it, pounding through the lamplit streets in the midst of a squad of provost guards, the soldiers who serve as the army's police, answering an urgent summons: a young private in a waterfront building had drawn a knife and killed another soldier in a fight over a woman. He had then barricaded himself in an upstairs room, claimed to have a pistol as well as the knife, and threatened to kill any one who approached unless he could talk to Reverend Brantley, Sherman's chaplain, the only one who would understand.

I prayed constantly as we sped along for the confidence and resilience that Christ alone can grant, knowing He will not give us more than we can handle, yet mortal enough to be plagued by anxiety. How crazed was this young private? How murderous? He had asked for me, for my help, and I took some reassurance in that, and gained even more reassurance when we rode by Saint Thomas with its reminder of Dorothea and her pistol. Protection had been granted then and, more important, the means to help those in need.

The dark and tranquil bulk of the church itself eased my spirit still more. Moonlight reflected in the stained glass, while across the lane in the vicarage, a lamp gleamed in the room where Reverend Witherspoon and I had talked. I pictured him quietly reading or working on next Sunday's sermon and felt not a touch of envy. I was where God wanted me, I told myself.

A few streets later, the neighborhood changed from tree-lined and luxurious to barren and mean and we clattered into the waterfront quarter, our horses' hooves sliding on the rutted thoroughfares. The jostling and pushing and shouting queues of men surrounded us, the perverse fairground I mentioned earlier, although we weren't slowed down. Despite some cursing, they parted smoothly at our approach, the way infantrymen routinely do for their cavalry, an ingrained habit of these battle veterans.

There was no shouting in the next street, only hushed whispering as men, and some women, crowded up to a semi-circle of rifle-bearing provost guards posted around a grimy brick building, two floors high, bearing a "Billiards and Saloon" sign above the door.

As we rode through, a voice called out, "He's a good boy, Chaplain," and another called, "Don't let them shoot him," surprising me. I had expected anger at a soldier who killed one of his fellows. Instead, scanning the faces when I dismounted, I found only concern.

A waiting lieutenant hurried me inside, past the bar and through rows of billiard tables, to a staircase where Major Nims took my arm and informed me the young soldier, Tom Watkins by name, was in a room upstairs, that the man he killed was his best friend and that the woman they fought over was also in the room, taken hostage. If Watkins heard anybody but me on the stairs, he would use his pistol on them.

The complication of a woman captive, another life at risk, revived my anxiety, leading to a grim expression that Major Nims misunderstood.

"I can't ask you to go up there unarmed," he said. "We can storm the room, do our best to spare the woman—"

"No Major, I'm prepared to go." I removed my coat to make it clear I carried no concealed weapon, took a lamp handed to me by a guard and and started up, calling out, "Tom! Tom Watkins! It's Chaplain Brantley. I'm coming up the stairs. I'm alone. I'm glad you sent for me. I want to talk to you."

At the top, I confronted an open space to my right that held an assortment of mismatched tables and chairs and a sagging divan. To my left stood a pine-board wall with curtained entrances to rooms beyond. Obviously, I was in a hastily assembled trysting arena, repugnant to begin with and made even more so by lingering tobacco smoke and whiskey odors. The nearest curtains parted to reveal the haggard face of a boy no more than seventeen or eighteen.

He looked suspiciously down the stairs, then stepped out for a closer look, a Bowie knife in his hand.

The thought, 'Show no fear and be firm,' came into my head and, having asked the Lord to lead me, I said sharply, "Tom! You heard me tell you I was coming up the stairs alone. Do you trust me? Or do I go back down and let the provost deal with you?"

"No, no," he murmured, his body folding in as if the air had gone out of it, backing inside, arms hanging, knife dangling without threat. A girl in her teen years—at least that was my first impression—sat against the headboard of a bed along the wall, knees drawn up inside a bright lavender gown. Tom sat heavily on the end of the bed, arms clasped around his chest and I placed myself on a wooden chair, the only other item of furniture the small room could hold.

"This is Carla," Tom said, his voice shaking. "I think she's beautiful," he added, making it sound like an explanation. With the light closer, I could see that she was indeed pretty, older than I thought, perhaps in her early twenties, but with thick blonde curls and a fresh, youthful complexion. She showed neither fear nor anger and kept her eyes steadily fixed on Tom.

"She's had a difficult time, Tom. She must be very tired. If you like her, you should let her leave."

"I'll never see her again."

"Carla, you go downstairs now," I told her and she rose slowly—reluctantly, it seemed—bringing herself by the lamp I held, revealing a slackness of mouth and the wide-eyed, dark eyes of a five-year-old, still set on Tom.

Oh, poor girl, she's simple-minded. I almost said it aloud, watching her sit like a child on Tom's knees for a moment. When she parted the curtains to leave, she stepped out backwards, watching Tom until the curtains closed.

"Never," he repeated, then, "I have no friends now. They'll hate me, every one."

"The men outside are on your side. They still like you, Tom."

"Do they? Sure thing? You're not just trying to cheer me?"

"They shouted at us not to shoot you, that you were a good boy. They like you and want you to leave here safely. I feel the same way."

He started to cry at that, and words spilled out, a dam breached, unstoppable. "You see, they know me, I joined up as a drummer boy, fourteen years old, but at Fort Donelson we needed every man when the Rebs come out of the fort and attacked so I picked up a rifle and I been a fighting man three years now and Billy Kiernan was alongside me all the way, protecting me, me protecting him, and we were best friends as tight as you could find, two brothers couldn't a' been tighter."

He glanced side to side as if someone might overhear and leaned toward me. "And, Reverend, we, well, neither of us was ever with a woman before, and we got here to Savannah, everybody talking about—see, we both went to church and Sunday School, I can quote from Scripture a lot—everybody talking about the waterfront and all and we, we—gave in, just gave in and we come here and started to drink and we weren't used to it, more'n we ever drank before, and then Carla—we were downstairs and I met Carla and we just liked each other right off and went to a corner to talk, we were getting along so fine, and she said she loved me and she knew a room upstairs—I mean, Reverend, I was so, so—this beautiful girl—Reverend, I'm sobered up and I'm not a fool, I know what Carla does, but when she said she loved me I know she meant it, means it, can you believe that?"

"I believe it, Tom." In truth, I did think it was so, at least while she was with him. Whether she would remember it by tomorrow was questionable.

"But Billy Kiernan couldn't see it, though, or he never would've done what he did, carrying on about me taking the best-looking girl in the room and he would come upstairs, too, and he put his hand on Carla, where you shouldn't, so I pushed him and he tried to hit me—"

He looked at the knife, wiped it on his jacket and handed it to me.

"The pistol, Tom? Or were you just faking that?"

"Just faking, never had one. Will you help me?" he pleaded. "I really can quote from Scripture: 'I will forgive their iniquity and I will remember their sin no more.' That's the Lord speaking, in Jeremiah, right?"

"Jeremiah, yes, although there are psalms that might be even closer to what you want."

"I remember, I remember," he said. "'For thou, Lord, art good, and ready to forgive.' I can say it all if you'd help me."

"It's from Psalm Eighty-five." I sat next to him and put my arm around his shoulder and together we recited, "'For thou, Lord, art good and ready to forgive, and plenteous in mercy unto all them that call upon thee. Give ear, O Lord, unto my prayer, and attend to the voice of my supplications. In the day of my trouble I will call upon thee, for thou wilt answer me.'"

He stood up now, a small lad, smaller in reality than my anxiety had made him seem when he first parted the curtain, handsome now that the pinched look of fear had receded somewhat, a curly-haired youth with the healthy bloom of the countryside that no trouble can fully erase. Carla's reaction to him became clearer.

"They'll take me to the stockade now and then they'll

hang me, what they should do to a man that kills his best friend."

"I'll speak up for you, Tom."

"Will you? I deserve to hang and I ain't afraid to die, all the combat I been through, but truth is, I want to live. If I live, maybe I can find Carla after the war."

A quick image passed my mind of these two children-in-spirit actually making a life together, a small farm somewhere—preposterous idea, I know, preposterous.

Downstairs, Palmer had arrived and he, Major Nims and the guards listened intently as I explained everything, the guards gradually easing their rough grip on Tom and, when they led him out, it was without ropes or restraints.

I asked where Carla had gone and the major replied, "The hostage? We let her leave with a couple who said they were her parents." He shrugged at the probability of that being true. "She's backward, as you say, not much use at giving testimony and we have plenty of other witnesses."

In a few minutes, Palmer and I were alone and I gestured at the bar, saying, "I need to sit down and pray."

"Where the sinners gather?"

"Jesus would approve," I told him, perched on a bar stool for the first time in my life. I thanked the Lord for leading me tonight and asked for his sheltering hand over Tom, for protection for Carla, this lamb amid the jackals, and for His grace and mercy on those who were straying so far from the path in this city tonight.

Palmer joined me in "Amen" and then asked, "Do you recognize what happened tonight as another situation of your own making?"

"How can you say that? I was sent for by the provost himself!"

"I'm not being critical, no need to snap at me. I want you to see that you were sent for because you have established yourself as the one person in this army who could be sent for, who should be sent for. Your actions, from the time we took Hillardville, have set you apart."

"I've never taken action without feeling called to it by the Lord."

"And I've come to accept it, that you are convinced that you hear the Lord's call, and I'm even half-persuaded that you're right about it. It still leaves you so vulnerable—do you know why Sherman likes you?"

"I preach well, a gift from God. I try not to be vain about it."

"You preach powerfully. You'll be famous for it someday, if you live through this war, but that's not it. You remind Sherman of himself."

"That's absurd. I detest warfare."

"See things through Sherman's eyes: a general who plunges an army into five hundred miles of enemy territory, no supply lines, no communications, no reinforcements, just supreme confidence that he's doing the right thing, and a chaplain who chases after an old Negro into a town that might be full of enemy snipers, no escort, no weapons, no escape route, just supreme confidence that he's doing the right thing. I'll confess something to you. Once when I complained to him that you were reckless, a peril to yourself and others, he said, 'War is perilous,' and he smiled."

"He smiled?"

"Smiled, and I'll interpret that for you. After a thousand miles with him, I'm an expert. It means that if someone is going to be called Sherman's chaplain, this is the kind of chaplain he should be."

"Am I to be flattered by this?"

"If you wish," he said, sliding off the stool as the barman appeared and some patrons began to return. "If you wish. You'll keep on doing what you do in any event, won't you?"

"And you'll keep on being my watchdog. Why?"

He considered it, then said lightly, "You have your calling, I have mine."

Elaine, have I ever looked cynical? I think I did at that moment.

I must pause now, my love. The Cambridge has no regular chaplain so the skipper has taken advantage of my presence—I welcome it, of course—and I'm due to conduct a shipboard service. I will continue in the next letter.

With undying devotion, and with deep need of your prayers,

Ellis

January 6, 1865

Elaine, My Dearest,

We're passing Wilmington, NC, as I write, a port blockaded by our fleet, and the only visible traffic is a motionless Union cruiser exchanging flag signals with us. We sail close to shore, almost always within sight of it. Bare tree limbs and a whip-like chill to the sea air confirm we're sailing north. A ship's officer has loaned me a woolen navy jacket and a crewman has placed a tankard of what he called hot grog at my feet, although I know it's coffee. They've taken to friendly banter with me after just this one day aboard, a drop of cheer that's timely considering my melancholic state right now, which brings me, reluctantly, to resuming the narrative.

When Palmer and I stepped outside, the earlier hush of worry over Tom had evaporated and a milling crowd of men and women was breaking into different destinations: the billiards/saloon building behind us, the weatherbeaten houses along the street, the shadowed lanes between the houses, the cavernous storage sheds on the docks. The guard had left our horses at a hitching rail halfway up the street and we started to push our way through.

"You're going to draw some reactions" he said, and I did, the most common being a quick averting of the eyes along with a sudden need to cough or blow the nose, requiring a kerchief over the face. Countering that, however, were those who openly acknowledged me, looking deliberately, leaving the impression they were satisfied I was there. The looks were often long, the expressions shifting from somber to resigned, punctuated by little hand gestures of regret, all of which I read as, Yes, we know we're wrong and we intend to stop and seek forgiveness.

There were also some looks of determined defiance, to be expected. If Satan is going to be at work, this was surely the place.

The women showed no reaction. What's one more man in this carnival? They flaunted gowns of pink and green and lavender, like Carla's, a merry touch here in January contradicted, and pitiably so, by faces tired and puffy and so pale, like flour paste, that wide daubs of rouge only magnified it. Their movements, a sway of a hip or toss of a curl, meant to be enticing, were as mechanical as a clockwork figurine's and only the older ones even bothered. The younger ones, knowing they would command the most attention and the highest prices, made no effort and when I say younger ones, distressingly, I mean truly young. Palmer and I turned away from the sight of two girls no more than fourteen entering a doorway, followed by five grinning, unsteady soldiers.

The drinkers were out, too, in all their varieties—noisy, cheering, sullen, staggering—including one who stumbled blindly into Palmer as we neared the horses. Palmer grabbed his arms and maneuvered him to the side of a building, trying to ease him off his feet. At the same moment a sergeant, an old-timer I recognized as a faithful attender on Sunday morning, came from the crowd to face me.

He struggled for words, then blurted out, "We're far from home, Chaplain, you can understand it, can't you?"

"You're never far from God," flashed through my mind but it would have been a retort, not a response, and I said simply, "I understand it, Sergeant, I understand it. But isn't it time now to end this and return to camp?"

His eyes shifted over my shoulder and suddenly he backed against the hitching post, dragging me with him, away from a surly band of men swinging up the street, some with locked arms, some waving bottles, filling most of the thoroughfare with their challenge, forcing all to move away. In the vanguard strutted a thin and intense soldier with long hair and I peered closely. Was he the one who threatened me during Cleary's rescue? So many of this gang were disheveled, I couldn't be sure.

"They're nothing to worry about," said the sergeant, seeing me stare after them. "The provost will round them up when he's ready and they'll go along quiet enough. Otherwise, they'll hang for desertion"

"You know the streets around here, Sergeant?"

He hesitated. "Chaplain, I confess I've been in bad places—"

"No, that's not it. I have to know if there's a street parallel to this, one that would take me to the big church with the stained glass windows, you know the one I mean?"

He pointed. "Sure, go by the livery and turn north, take you right there."

I pulled my horse from the rail. Palmer, still wrestling the drunk into place, looked up.

"Brantley!"

I rode off, threading my way through the revelers until

I reached the quiet, well-tended streets, where I spurred the animal to a gallop. The route the hostile band had chosen was the one we had taken here, passing Saint Thomas, and if the long-haired one was the man I suspected he was, we were contending with a church-burner. I recalled the frenzied whoops of glee when they torched the church in Hillardville. With the moon high and bright now, they would be drawn like moths to the gleaming presence of Saint Thomas.

The lamp still burned in the vicarage and I knocked softly at the room's veranda door. Reverend Witherspoon went into his hawk stance at my words but listened carefully, then told me he had prepared the house with a cellar strong room when he first heard Sherman's army was coming. He would tell Mrs. Finch to lead everyone there and then he would stand at the church door. He thanked me for the warning as if I had come by only for that and would now ride off to safety.

"I'll be at the door with you, Reverend."

"A wild mob? There could be danger for you, no matter your uniform."

"A friend of mine, a captain, has found out by now where I am and he'll be here quickly, with provost guards."

"And until then?"

"We'll stand together. Would you deny me that?"

"If I could, yes." He vanished inside.

They came across the lawn in a straggling line, no more than a dozen of them, fewer than it appeared in the universal bedlam back at the waterfront and here, with their shouting and posturing and bottle-waving, they could have been stage extras at a comic opera.

Of course, they were not acting. They were drunk and unruly, their menace was focused instead of scattered among a crowd and their leader, no question about his identity now, was the long-haired soldier from Hillardville. He confronted us from thirty feet away, flanked by two equally unkempt companions, the rest moving into a tight knot behind them.

He studied me through an alcoholic haze, rubbed his forehead, then remembered.

"The preacher! Hey, here's the preacher took away that Rebel brat tried to shoot us!" His voice was high-pitched and screeching, grating on the ears. "You gonna keep us from burning this Reb church? You and the little fat fellow? Aren't no more monkey women around to help you! Come on boys, get some rocks, we'll start with them fancy windows!"

Reverend Witherspoon took a step forward and I held him back. My stomach was tight and I listened eagerly for the sound of hooves as I raised my arms and spoke out, guarding against fear in my voice and surprising myself by the dark anger that welled up instead.

"Go ahead," I bellowed. "Destroy this house of God! You can do it! We can't stop you!" I pointed to one, then another. "You! Pick up a rock! You! Light a torch! Why are you waiting? How about you, or you, or you? Are you afraid I'll get a good look at you? That God will get a good look at you? He already knows what's in your heart, and you will be judged. Oh, yes, you—will—be—judged!"

For a moment, it stopped them. They backed away by a step or two from the leader until he screamed at them, "It's a Rebel church! It's no house of your god nor mine! You gonna listen to this Rebel-lover? How many churches we burned already? God ever throw down a lightnin' bolt on one of us? Come on, come on, come on!"

Roused again, they responded with shouts of "Burn it down!" and one of them hurled a rock that caromed off the ledge below the stained glass. Torches were lit and they moved forward, then paused at the sight of Palmer riding at a slow trot across the grass, erect and stately in the saddle, treating the church lawn as a parade ground.

Dismounting, still without hurry, he handed the reins to one of the mob with a curt, "Hold this horse steady, soldier." He stood before them without a word, immobile as a statue in the moonlight. Torches were extinguished, rocks replaced on the ground, shoulders drawn straighter, unsteady hands dropped into a semblance of the military attention stance.

The leader alone remained defiant, turning in silent appeal first to one, then the other of the two companions who still flanked him, getting only cautionary glances in reply. He examined the rest of his followers and received the same reaction. He began to shift from one foot to the other, mouth twisted, hands actually quivering in rage.

I compared Palmer's results with my ineffectual bellowing and understood there were depths to Palmer that were apparent to the troops but not to me, an aura of authority and a moral rectitude that I had missed, reacting as I had only to his displays of sarcasm at our early meetings. Watching him now, standing as he had the night we buried the Rebel boys, I conceded that I hadn't heard any sarcasm since then. I scolded myself for not taking the time to know this man better.

Riders were heard approaching and Palmer broke his silence. "Those are provost guards, coming to arrest you. Give them no trouble, and I will speak to the provost marshal in your behalf. You will be charged only with breaking company regulations and your punishment will be some extra duty, no stockade time."

There were murmurs of relief, except for the long-haired one, who continued quivering and glaring at me.

Lowering his voice, Palmer told me, "Just look away. That's Corsey, half-crazy and getting worse lately, but when you need someone to lead a bayonet charge, you're happy to have him." He looked to Reverend Witherspoon. "Is this the priest here?"

I introduced them and the reverend said, "Very courageous chaplain you have, sir. The Union army needs more like him."

"Courageous and reckless. This is the most foolish thing you've done yet, Brantley, charging off when I was right there. How long would it have taken to call out to me? I would have been with you instantly, we would have picked up guards along the way, the danger here to you and to Reverend Witherspoon would have been avoided."

"The church—I didn't think I had any time to spare. I pictured it in ruins."

"Yes, yes, it's a house of God, a beautiful one, a classic—"

He waved his arm at it and then he was on the ground, Reverend Witherspoon kneeling over him and I was heading for Corsey, murder in my heart, still trying to grasp that I had heard an uncontrolled scream of rage and the hard clap of a pistol—

The pistol was on the ground, knocked down by one of Corsey's companions. "You shot the captain, you shot the captain," he said incredulously to Corsey.

"Him!" Corsey screeched, pointing at me. "Him! I aimed at him! He's the one started the trouble! You had'na pushed me, I'd a' shot him!"

Corsey's companions now had him in in their grip and provost guards were tearing across the lawn. I took a long breath, simultaneously asking the Lord to ease the fury that no mortal should feel, certainly not one of His servants.

I ran back to where Palmer lay, in time to hear Reverend Witherspoon intoning soft words.

"...and let perpetual light shine upon him. May his soul and the souls of all the faithful departed, through the mercy of God..."

I cannot go on at this point, Elaine.

Pray for me,
Ellis

January 7, 1865

My Dearest Elaine,

A night has elapsed since my last letter and I can resume now. I'll post these last three letters together when we dock at Norfolk, only a few hours away, so you'll receive the whole narrative as one. Now that I will be in one place, I can receive answering letters from you. How welcome that will be!

It was known the next morning that I would be transferred. Even before Sherman's messenger brought me the orders and a summons to meet the general at noon, Lambert, in his usual way, had picked up the news from his friends at headquarters.

"Uncle Billy's real upset. His orderly says he's pacing around like a wolf in a cage. But you talked to him before, just the two of you. Maybe you could quiet him down, change his mind." He looked at me questioningly.

"He has no choice," I said. "My effectiveness here is at an end. Nobody will be able to look at me without thinking of Captain Palmer. Every sermon I preach, every prayer meeting I hold, every word I speak will be poisoned by that. I have to leave."

"I suppose." He fumbled for more, then concluded, "I suppose."

"The men aren't angry with you," Samuel Ward told me, watching Lambert start to pack my belongings.

"Well, there's a few," corrected Silas.

"Wouldn't count them," Samuel argued. "The hotheads, would they like him whatever he did?"

"Guess not," Silas conceded. "He makes them too uncomfortable."

"What do most of the men feel then, sorrow?" I asked.

They both weighed that, then Silas answered, "About as close as you can get, I guess, sorrow. You see, they respect you for saving Tom Watkins like you did, but against that, there's the church—"

"They know you got gumption," Samuel cut in, "facing up to Corsey and that bunch."

"No question about that," Silas agreed, "but you rushed in to save a Rebel church and a Rebel priest and that bothers a lot of them."

"Even though it's the church and the priest who are helping Dorothea and Barbara and little Silas?"

"That goes into the, the stew I guess you'd call it, everything all mixed together in their thinking."

"Never had something like this to puzzle through," Samuel added. "So if you want to call it one thing or another, sorrow'll probably do. As for us, me and Silas, the way we think about it—"

"He asked me before if we could transfer to Norfolk," Silas said, "and he was only half-joking."

The Savannah city jail had been commandeered as the stockade and the provost sergeant serving as jailer pointed me to the corridor, where Tom was sweeping the floor. There was no point in locking him up, decent boy that he was, and where's he gonna run to, anyhow?

Tom told me Major Nims thought he would get a two-year sentence and be able to serve most of it at the army stockade in Cairo, Illinois, near his home, once the war was over. Tom's baffling suggestion that he stay here in the Savannah jail was rejected. The Union army would be gone once peace was declared.

"I'll have to get a job when I get out and save some money and then come back here. You figure Carla might be married to someone else by then?"

I said we should pray for wisdom and we went to his cell, where the door was wide open. The guards had given him a tattered little Bible left by some previous prisoner. Tom knew Job Twenty-eight, in which Job asks where wisdom is to be found and we read that together, then prayed for wisdom for Tom and, again, for forgiveness for what he had done.

Corsey was locked securely in a cell with a guard posted, although the prisoner was curled on the floor in a corner, eyes clouded and unseeing, evidently plied with some opiate. On my way out, the sergeant said an army doctor and a Savannah city doctor had been called in this morning and had agreed there must be a growth inside the brain, something malignant that was expanding rapidly.

He'll hang, said the sergeant, a military court would show no mercy to someone who shot an officer, so there's a cure for him.

Sherman and about two dozen staff officers were sitting in a circle in a vast, chandeliered ball room—I mentioned earlier that headquarters was in a cotton broker's mansion—with maps and dispatches spread on the floor. The officers looked at me with curiosity or, validating the Ward brothers, with a touch of sorrow. A few nodded to me sympathetically. Sherman's expression turned harsh, however, and he motioned me into a small parlor.

When the door closed, our eyes met and a quick softening came to his face, a reaction uncontrollable even for this obdurate man. The last time we had been alone was to mourn his infant son and the silent acknowledgment of that link passed between us. An instant later, the harshness returned.

"Did you know the priest from Saint Thomas was here this morning? Did you put him up to it?"

"I didn't know, sir, and he's not the sort of man who can be put up to anything."

"Stubborn, yes. He came here to offer his church cemetery for Captain Palmer's burial and I agreed. He also wanted to perform the service and I refused. I told him you, and only you, should do that. You'll be branded a coward if you don't say the last words over a fallen companion. The men expect it; they've done it so often themselves. Are you prepared for that?"

"Yes, sir."

"Good. Now let's state the obvious: you cost me one of my best officers and it should have been avoided."

"I know, sir."

"I'm as angry at myself as I am at you. I let you get out of hand. Palmer kept warning me. I hope you understand that he was a friend to you, a protector."

"I came to realize that."

"But I liked the idea of a daring young chaplain on my staff so I didn't listen, didn't think it through. I overlooked your youth, just how unaware you might be that boldness goes hand in hand with calculation: when is it effective? When is it destructive?"

Turning to grasp the doorknob, he continued, "When you go to Norfolk, you will no longer have the freedom you enjoyed here. I wrote to the commanding general this morning and informed him you were gifted but impetuous. I instructed him that you were to serve as a regimental chaplain only, that you were not to be granted any additional authority, that you were to serve your own assigned regiment and no other and that you were to perform customary chaplain duties, nothing else. I also suggested a senior officer be appointed to review your daily schedule to insure compliance. Can you handle this?"

"Yes, sir."

He opened the door and returned to his meeting.

"Think of it as your first church."

Reverend Witherspoon and I sat on a knoll overlooking the Savannah River east of the city, at a point where it splits in two around an island, the current quickening as it nears the ocean, ships visibly moving faster, reminding me of how little time there was before I would be aboard the Cambridge, sailing to Norfolk.

The Saint Thomas cemetery spread out around the

knoll, deserted now after my second burial service of the morning. Billy Kiernan's was first, in a dell north of the city where his company was camped and where they had found a secluded point sheltered by stunted oak trees. Tom Watkins was kept away for fear he would break down but he had gotten a message to his sergeant, a request that I read Psalm Thirty-four, which I did, pausing before and after the verse I knew he wanted me to stress: "The Lord is nigh unto them that are of a broken heart, and saveth such as be of a contrite spirit."

Billy's funeral had been attended only by his company, most of them hidden from my view by the trees. Palmer's was attended by a large crowd, all visible in the open cemetery ground, and their numbers were about equally divided between our military and members of the Saint Thomas congregation. Sherman was present, of course, and I wondered if it crossed his mind, as it did mine, that this much, at least, was achieved by Palmer's death: a public demonstration that a Yankee soldier could be a defender as well as an attacker and that enemies could be brought together.

My service was short, built around words from Romans, Chapter Eight—"Who shall separate us from the love of Christ?"—to underscore the point that we are all His children, all one in His sight.

I praised Palmer's career, his bravery in battle, his martydom at the church and then, if the onlookers expected a personal note from me, they were not disappointed. As the coffin lowered, I said, "This grave will hold a better friend than I knew; a better friend than I deserved." If they expected tears, they were disappointed. My thoughts were too deep for tears.

"Simply think of it as your first church," Reverend Witherspoon repeated. "You'll have the same soldiers week after week, you'll come to know their individual needs, you'll be able to pray with them, to console them when necessary. They will become your congregation and that's a fine thing. If you can't roam free any more, it will allow you to concentrate on your congregation and you'll be surprised at the great variety of challenges and satisfactions you'll have."

He smiled slyly and went on, "And your church will be in a barracks or warehouse, your altar probably an empty rifle crate, all the simplicity of surroundings you could ask for."

I smiled in turn, the first time in two days.

"You know," he continued, "the irony is not lost on me. You risked your life for a church building you don't like."

"We preach from the same Book. The surroundings are less important to me now than they were. And congregations do rebuild churches."

"Indeed. It's happening right now from Chattanooga to Atlanta and will no doubt be happening through the Carolinas after your General Sherman finishes with them."

"Meeting with him must have been difficult for you."

"We were civil but all I could see in his face was war. I'm pleased that you're no longer his chaplain."

I watched an army wagon rattle down the cemetery road: Lambert with my belongings, ready to take me to the harbor.

"I'm pleased, too," I said.

The Cambridge is slowing now and starting a wide turn toward land. The sea is calm, the day clear enough so that long low buildings just north of the harbor can be made out—army barracks? A regiment waiting for its chaplain?

They'll be getting one eager to be their chaplain, one who craves no higher post, one who wants to learn how to help them, how to minister to them.

They'll also be getting a chaplain who's struggling, still searching for his own peace.

I see myself rushing headlong to St. Thomas that night, knowing Palmer would follow me. He did and he died there. God allowed it, yes, but was it His will that sent me or a prideful delusion?

I had just come from a triumph with Tom Watkins and Carla, just listened to Palmer tell me I was the only one who could have managed it, just walked through a crowd of people treating me with open respect, just had a sergeant, a man older than I by many years, beseeching me for understanding. Was I truly reading God's will or riding a self-image as some knight-errant, a Galahad to the rescue?

And all the previous episodes—was my high-sounding role as Sherman's chaplain blinding me to the difference between my own choices and God's commands?

In Hillardville, William found his way to Rosella on his own. My help with Cleary? Rosella was prepared to get him to the hospital without me. Dorothea and the children? The Wards would have saved them one way or another; these brothers don't give up. And Jonathan Raymond, the dying Rebel boy? There was no shortage of dying boys that terrible day. Had I been with the headquarters unit, my proper post, I might have ministered to a dozen such boys.

And yet, the one lost sheep—you thought of it instantly, didn't you? Among all of them was Jonathan the boy the Lord wanted to reach with His word? Had he sent Jonathan stumbling away from the battle just when I rode back from the hospital so we might meet at that particular time and place?

And William: was his faith wavering under the weight

of that drum? Did I help restore it? Or Dorothea? After a life-shattering night, a clergyman with a Bible appears—a sign? God has not abandoned you? Cleary and Anita—they were resentful to the end but were seeds planted to blossom later? And my preaching at the field hospital, where they welcomed a chaplain: did hearing the gospel re-direct a life that morning?

And then, Palmer.

Yes, Palmer.

Did he die because God wanted that church building preserved? Was God using him to protect those in the vicarage from fire or attack by the mob? Was it His purpose that Palmer's sacrifice keep me alive for some work in the future?

And on and on...a tapestry of infinite threads, moving and shifting; grasping one thread reveals nothing of its influence at some other point, some other moment. But in this endless mystery, so clear to God, so perplexing to us, can I know that I have grasped the thread He wants me to?

Standing at the rail the first night at sea, pondering this, a childhood memory came to me. In Sunday Bible classes, I received the highest marks week after week. One Sunday, when my father asked how I had done, I answered "First place, of course," in a tone that meant, "What else could it be?"

The lecture that followed was memorable. Pride poisons our minds, pride bewitches our senses, pride makes us deaf and blind to God's will. Only the humble heart will drive pride away, only the humble heart will open our ears and eyes to His leading, only the humble heart will make us His true servants.

Yes, yes, yes—and still, when I preach and I see people are roused, no matter how much I give God the praise, there's that child inside that whispers, Ellis, you did it, lad.

Being appointed headquarters chaplain for the commanding general of all our Southern armies—how can that lurking child not break into a secret little grin?

Isn't that what sent me charging off to St. Thomas without calling for help, without thinking about God's will?

But Palmer's death humbles me as nothing before in my life. Imagine contemplating it, learning to accept it, during three days and three nights in the vastness of the sea, where even an eight hundred ton ship feels like a twig adrift. How can I not be humbled?

We've come into the harbor now, sailing ships and steamers and barges all around us, docks crowded with lounging seamen, workers loading and unloading cargo, steady lines of wagons carrying goods in, taking goods away, rifle-bearing soldiers patrolling the walkways, a reminder there's still a war to be waged—although probably not for much longer. The general opinion is that by April, one Union army will be in Petersburg and the other in Raleigh, leaving Lee in between with nothing to do but surrender.

If they're right, we'll be together in four or five months and you know how I ache for that. One of the countless things I treasure about you is that lovingly critical eye you cast on me at those times when I need it. Never stop. If I ever bridle at it, please, Elaine, look at me levelly and seriously, and say two words: "Sherman's chaplain."

With love and devotion forever,
Ellis

www.ingramcontent.com/pod-product-compliance
Lightning Source LLC
Chambersburg PA
CBHW051851170626
46807CB00003B/1435